Mobility, Modernity, and Space
in
Jane Eyre, Villette,
and
North and South

ISHII Marie

KINSEIDO

Mobility, Modernity, and Space
in *Jane Eyre*, *Villette*, and *North and South*
by ISHII Marie

Copyright©2024 by ISHII Marie

ISBN978-4-7647-1235-5

For Kyoko and Kenji ISHII, my parents

Acknowledgements

This book is based on my doctoral thesis undertaken at Meiji Gakuin University.

First and foremost, I am extremely grateful to Prof. Dr. Satoshi Ando, my PhD thesis supervisor, and Prof. Dr. Michael Pronko, and Associate Prof. Dr. Paul Hullah, my PhD thesis sub-chief examiners for their time and effort, and for providing valuable feedback. Their insights and suggestions have greatly enriched the quality of my work.

Furthermore, I would like to express my gratitude to Emeritus Prof. Dr. Kazuhiko Funakawa of Sophia University. Since I was a graduate student at Sophia University, he has given me treasured support and continuous encouragement. Thanks to him, I have had the opportunity to publish this book.

Finally, I wish to thank my parents. Their support and belief in me have provided me with strength and motivation. Without their constant understanding, patience, and love, I could not have accomplished this academic journey.

Contents

Introduction 1

Chapter 1
Space, Gendered Space, and Mobility 11
   1.1. Space and Gendered Space 11
   1.2. Heterotopia (Michel Foucault) 15
   1.3. Mobility 18

Chapter 2
Walking and Mobility 23
   2.1. *Jane Eyre* 24
      2.1.1. Walking 24
      2.1.2. Travel by Coach and Stagecoach 38
   2.2. *Villette* 44
      2.2.1. Walking 44
      2.2.2. Travel by Coach and by Sea 65
   2.3. *North and South* 75
      2.3.1. Walking 75
      2.3.2. Travel by Rail and Coach 98

Chapter 3
Transformation and Identity 111
   3.1. *Jane Eyre* 113
   3.2. *Villette* 136
   3.3. *North and South* 157

Conclusion 177
Works Cited 199

Introduction

Nineteenth-century Britain witnessed the development of a new mobile culture and society. The transport revolution and improved streets increased people's mobility on foot, by coach, and by rail and led to the emergence of new purposes for journeys, which were embarked on for pleasure and health, work and necessity, success and wealth. Many novelists recognised travel as a structural, thematic, and representational device in their works, and consequently, travelling, voyaging, and other forms of journey became a significant component in the characters' development.

Since the 1970s, scholars in sociology and geography have redefined the concept of space. For example, Henri Lefebvre argues that space is a social product in his work, *The Production of Space*. Doreen Massey, furthering Lefebvre's concept, described space as "the product of interrelations as constituted through interactions, from the immensity of the global to the intimately tiny" (9). Thus, space always interacts with social relations and its interactive relation is flexible. Simultaneously, feminist geographers and feminists have begun to analyse the male-centred perspective in society and have demonstrated that patriarchy, the law of the father, contributes towards constructing a definition of space where men are superior to women. According to Linda McDowell, "in advanced industrial societies there are several ways in which this superiority and control is constructed and enforced" (16). Leslie Kanes Weisman, a feminist architect examining the social utilisation of space and the oppression of women, argues that in a patriarchal society, men, as the dominant group, have owned the absolute power to define and control space. Consequently, the social, physical, and metaphorical spaces are, as Weisman argues, "the products of male experience, male consciousness, and male control" (10). Such hierarchical relationships shape a specific discourse of spatial usages based on gender and class norms, which is clearly demonstrated by the ideology of "separate spheres", whereby women (especially middle-class women in the Victorian Age) were restricted to the private sphere, while men were free to move between the domestic and public spheres. Thus, the spatial division between the public and the private, between inside and outside, has a central role in the social construction of gender divisions.

Certainly, it is difficult to conceive how the home could provide such a strict barrier from the barbarisms and secularities of the outer world. According to Andrea Kaston Tange, imagining the domestic sphere as the complete opposite of the public sphere was a middle-class society's "desire" (12). Leonore Davidoff and Catherine Hall argue that "as the spatial and temporal quarantine between the public and the private grew, they were ever more identified with gender" (319). However, Eleanor Gordon, Mary Poovey, and Dorice Williams Elliott stress women's engagement with the public sphere and their possibilities of utilising their domestic skills outside the house in charitable and educational works, which consequently blurred the public/private and male/female distinctions. Additionally, as Wendy Parkins claims, "freedom of movement was implicitly associated with property rights and political entitlements" (2009; 2). Nineteenth-century England experienced a lot of political, social, economic, and cultural shifts, including industrialisation, urbanisation, and increasing democratisation, which had a major influence on women's roles and gender identities. Many women no longer stayed home and fled from their houses to seek new places, opportunities, and jobs, often by moving to the urban areas. In nineteenth-century literature, we can see several female characters travelling on foot, by stagecoach, and by train to find a new place to belong to and build their space. I contend that mobility in Victorian novels plays a central role in exploring the new and changing relationship between the individual and space. Mobility opens up new perspectives to the characters, including regions, class, gender, time, and modernity, which makes it possible to produce a new space. However, while modernisation expanded the range of women's access to places, space, journeys and mobility, it also introduced new physical and psychological anxieties to women.

This study aims to deliberately trace the space the protagonists in the selected novels produce through their mobility in a world which had just begun to experience modernity. Additionally, it analyses how the protagonists, as middle-class women, negotiated with the social norms of class or gender. Furthermore, the study attempts to clarify how these aspects contributed to the development of the protagonists' identities. According to Tim Cresswell, an English geographer, "identities are produced and performed through mobility" (44). This argument strongly suggests to me that the protagonists have the possibilities to discover or build their own identities by experiencing various negotiations with new circumstances through mobility. Furthermore, Anthony Giddens, a sociologist, argues that "experiencing the body is a way of cohering the self as an integrated whole" (78). This suggests that the heroine's mobility including the experience of the body offers her the space to consider the self and sustain or produce her identity. Based on these recent arguments, this study examines the relationship of the middle-class woman's space, mobility, and identity in the modernising society.

The selected novels, *Jane Eyre* (1847) and *Villette* (1853) by Charlotte Brontë, and *North and South* (1854–55) by Elizabeth Gaskell, were published during the 1840s and 1850s—a period that witnessed great developments not only in transportation but also in the sensibilities of women, who were involved in industrialisation, urbanisation (due to people's mobility), and modernity. The works of Brontë and Gaskell have been chosen as the subject of this study as they are well-known female writers, who demonstrated a distinguished and strong interest in the illustration of independent women's 'space' in the changing Victorian society. While nineteenth-century British society was characterised by the Victorian ideology of separate spheres, and inequality between men and women, these writers created characters who challenged the societal norm. Embedded in a strictly patriarchal society, Brontë and Gaskell were not indifferent to these gendered dichotomies and social shifts and courageously unearthed the new relationship between women and their space, identity, and modernity.

The three novels were selected based on how the woman's (protagonist's) mobility affects the construction of space; how their space interacts with a society, which had gender, class, and age restrictions but was nevertheless progressing towards modernity; and how the woman establishes her identity through her interaction with society and through her mobility. Two works by Charlotte Brontë are selected because *Jane Eyre* and *Villette* present decidedly different productions of space and identity created by the protagonists' transgressions as mobile characters, who destabilise the normative dichotomy of separate spheres. I explore the literary spaces represented in the three works to articulate not only their spatial transgression but also their negotiation with the "acceptable" as per Victorian moral standards.

Charlotte Brontë's *Jane Eyre* illustrates a woman's quest for identity and independence. Since the time of its publication, *Jane Eyre* has attracted enormous interests among many critics in terms of its literary space. The novel has achieved a cult status within women's studies and feminist criticism, especially since the publication of *The Madwoman in the Attic*, in which Sandra M. Gilbert and Susan Gubar notably argue that the four locales depicted in the narrative suggest the four different hardships that "every woman in a particular society must meet and overcome": oppression, starvation, madness, and coldness (339). Conversely, in the introduction to the Oxford World Classics edition, Sally Shuttleworth focuses on the character's psychological interior space rather than geography. She argues, "selfhood in *Jane Eyre* is defined primarily as a hidden interior space, rather than a process of social interaction and exchange. It is in the hidden 'recesses of the heart' that the real action takes place", which should be "carefully guarded against intruders" (vii). Thus, several critics agree that Jane's story is more than a travelogue. While they have explored the narrative's settings as metaphors for stages in the heroine's personal journey and development, I contend that tracing Jane's construction of space through mobility might clarify how she interacts with society and builds her own identity.

Villette, Brontë's last novel, published seven years after *Jane Eyre*, creates a more psychologically complicated protagonist by reflecting the Victorian conception of the liminal woman. Liana F. Piehler argues that in *Villette*, "spaces consistently loom vividly as recollections, memories, and dreams; as correlatives for inner personal spaces, thoughts…and as realizations of the self. Lucy's narrative becomes a creation and claiming of both space and self" (43). Like *Jane Eyre*, *Villette* demonstrates that it is difficult for a woman without fortune and family connection to build her place and identity. Setting the locale in a fictional, foreign metropolitan city, *Villette* offers the heroine a more complicated and problematic mobility and presents more nuanced insights into the construction of space in modern society.

Robert Burroughs argues that "as a writer of places, Elizabeth Gaskell's critical and popular reputation is based on her fictions of the city, provincial town, and countryside" (12). Gaskell's preoccupation towards places and spaces can be seen in *North and South*, which is another famous bildungsroman and also an industrial novel set in the Victorian age. As Divya Athmanathan mentions, it is a narrative that "juxtaposes the domesticities in the North and the South, the country and the town, the country and the forest, and the town and the suburbs" (37). Depicting Margaret Hale's development and maturation as she confronts difficulties, *North and South* simultaneously challenges both the societal problems caused by class struggle between masters and working people and the gendered spatial dichotomy.

Brontë and Gaskell explore similar authorial interests in these three novels: the gendered spatial dichotomy, the tension of class, the spatial contrast between the industrial town and the rural area, and individual autonomy. The authors set their narratives at the turning point in the history of transport, when both women's and men's mobility became more acceptable and easier, which expanded the possibility of the relationship between mobility and modernity. As Marshall Berman argues, "modern environments and experiences cut across all boundaries of geography and ethnicity, of class and nationality, of religion and ideology" (15). Brontë and Gaskell's heroines blur class and gender segregations built inside and outside the house by frequently moving between them, adapting and transforming themselves in modernised environments, and constituting an identity that differed from the typical feminine identity of the Victorian age. Subsequently, I will focus on the heroines' physical and psychological journey to clarify how they use space with their inclination towards modernity. I think that analysing Brontë and Gaskell's works is crucial for understanding women's physical and psychological spaces in the nineteenth century. It is well-known that Brontë and Gaskell's similar novelistic concerns allowed them to cultivate a deep friendship; write numerous letters to each other; and professionally, culturally, and personally exchange opinions in person. Gaskell read *Jane Eyre*, *Shirley*, *Villette*, and *The Professor*, and Brontë read *Mary Barton* while she was composing *Shirley*, as well as *Cranford*, *Ruth*, and part of *North and South*. Gaskell's *The Life of Charlotte Brontë*, published after her friend's death, perhaps most significantly demonstrates the strong links between the two famous Victorian female authors. These connections reveal their authorial influence on each other and signal the textual interactions between their works. Furthermore, the fact that Gaskell named some of her settings after the names of characters in Brontë's works demonstrates Gaskell's special interest in the space and the individual created by Brontë.

This study consists of an introduction, three main chapters, and a conclusion. The first chapter provides a theoretical basis for the definitions of the term "space" to explore the selected novels' social and literary space. This study is based on Henri Lefebvre's concept of spaces as a social product (*The Production of Space*, 1974) and utilises Linda McDowell's understanding of female geography as stated in *Gender,*

Identity and Place (1999), Judith Butler's argument of the subversion of identity (*Gender Trouble*, 1990) and Michel Foucault's concept of space ('Of Other Spaces', 1967). Moreover, I provide a brief introduction to the theorisation of mobility, which has recently been defined by social scientists and geographers: mobility is interpreted as a social product. According to Charlotte Mathieson, "the focus on space and its production is central to the theorization of mobility" (14). Based on these geographical, philosophical, and cultural theories, this study examines how the protagonists produce social and private spaces through their mobility and interactions with society, people, regions, and modernity.

The second chapter explores the representations of women's mobility, the mobile body, and space, which are constructed through interaction with movement. Walking is the primary means of mobility for the heroines in *Jane Eyre*, *Villette*, and *North and South*. In *Walking, Literature, and English Culture*, Anne D. Wallance claims that walking as a pleasurable mode of transportation is a relatively recent phenomenon, which emerged at the end of the eighteenth century. Prior to that, pedestrian travellers had to contest with bad roads, poor maps, and uncomfortable modes of transportation. Thus, as walking was associated with criminals, outlaws, and the poor, the writers in those days avoided writing about the painful progress of getting to the destination. However, as Robert Macfarlane argues in *Mountains of the Mind*, for certain types of people, at least, walking became a means of obtaining pleasure in the early eighteenth century. Romanticism, in particular, recognised walking as pastoral, reflecting the growing doubts and anxieties about writers' and readers' disconnective tendencies pertaining to modern technology. According to Charlotte Mathieson, in the early nineteenth century, as in *Pride and Prejudice* by Jane Austen, even if Elizabeth Bennet's long walk is considered wild, her social or sexual reputation is not undermined. However, "as the century progresses", the social trend goes in the direction of a "cultural discourse denigrating female mobility" (Mathieson 29). In this societal background, Brontë and Gaskell depict walking as a means for their heroines to find solace for their depression. Walking itself serves as their adventure; Jane, Lucy, and Margaret enjoy walking and walk with excitement in the town or city, full of changes and activities. Nevertheless, they must negotiate with gender identities regarding female mobility assigned by the Victorian middle-class norm, or boldly transgress them. In the selected novels, walking allows women to participate in the previously unexperienced community and public sphere, which leads to meditation and self-discovery; however, it also awakens the sensibility of loneliness and awareness regarding their fragile social position. In this chapter, I examine how, throughout their journeys, on foot, the mobile and restless protagonists in the selected novels reveal their inclination or declination toward modernity, in which people experienced the shifting of time and space. This chapter also examines women's journeys by coach, ship, and train—the new forms of transport introduced into nineteenth-century society, which often enhances the women's nostalgic affections for the past and their places in the past.

The third chapter explores the shifting of women's identities through the experience of restriction, mobility, modernity, and space produced by interaction with society. The deliberate and cautious efforts by the authors to describe the protagonists' transgressive speech and movement as middle-class women in the Victorian age are seen throughout the selected novels. As Tim Cresswell argues, identities are created and practiced through mobility. Therefore, I will explore how the mobile protagonists in the selected novels produce and discover their own identities through their private and social mobility.

This study seeks to clarify the relationship between mobility, modernity, space, and identity through the locus of the protagonist's body and the produced and embodied spaces constituted by her movement and travel. New critical understandings of mobility can be perceived from studies on the literature of the eighteenth and nineteenth centuries, such as *Mobility in the Victorian Novel* (2015) by Charlotte Mathieson. She focuses on the process of production of the nation—Great Britain—through the mobility of characters in some Victorian novels. In *Mobility and Modernity in Women's Novels, 1850s–1930s: Women Moving Dangerously* (2008), Wendy Parkins argues that the representations of mobility offer insights into the location of women within modernity and the opportunities for women's agency. In *Woman Wanderers and the Writing of Mobility, 1784–1844* (2017), Ingrid Horrocks points out that a woman's wandering in those days had the possibility of both freedom and sympathy. This study is indebted to these recent critical works, which have inspired me to examine the relationship between women and space produced through mobility. This study aims to trace how the protagonists, as women living in the Victorian era facing modernity, realised and produced their space through negotiated and contested mobility in society, and to explore how they discovered or established their own identities in modernity. The nexus of mobility-modernity-identity interrelations constitutes the key representational theme of this study.

CHAPTER 1
Space, Gendered Space, and Mobility

1.1. Space and Gendered Space

Michel Foucault, the renowned French philosopher, claimed in 1967 that "the present epoch will perhaps be above all the epoch of space. We are in the epoch of simultaneity: we are in the epoch of juxtaposition, the epoch of the near and the far, of the side-by-side, of the dispersed" (1998; 237). Foucault clarified the importance of space by claiming that we exist in a world of simultaneity—a juxtaposed world rather than a chronological world. Daphne Spain, a sociologist, also claimed that "space is essential to social science; spatial relations exist only because social processes exist; and the spatial and social aspects of a phenomenon are inseparable" (5).

This first chapter provides a theoretical background to space and gendered space. The analysis of the literary space is premised on the geographical insight that space is produced by social practices and forces. Henri Lefebvre, a classic Marxist sociologist, states the following about space in his work, *The Production of Space* (1974):

> (Social) space is not a thing among other things, nor a product among other products: rather, it subsumes things produced, and encompasses their interrelationships in their coexistence and simultaneity—their (relative) order and/or (relative) disorder. It is the outcome of the

> sequence and set of operations, and thus cannot be reduced to the rank of a simple object. At the same time there is nothing imagined, unreal or 'ideal' about it as compared, for example, with science, representations, ideas or dreams. Itself the outcome of past actions, social space is what permits fresh actions to occur, while suggesting others and prohibiting yet others. (73)

Thus, space is a social product, not a container or a vessel. Lefebvre emphasises that space is constructed by social practice and social relations. Moreover, Lefebvre conceives space as not only "a tool of thought and of action" and "a means of production" but also "a means of control, and hence of domination, of power" (26). That is, space produces the relationships between the oppressors and the oppressed. Based on Lefebvre's concept of space, Linda McDowell, a feminist geographer, argues that the binary gender division, which feminists have analysed, is implicated in "the social production of space", in the assumptions that the "environments" were built to be "natural", and in "the sets of regulations that influence who should occupy which spaces and who should be excluded" (11). McDowell, like other feminist geographers, regards "the body" as "the place, the location or site … of the individual" (34) within the socially constructed space by conceiving bodies as material that takes up space. Feminist scholars have demonstrated that women and femininity are defined as "irrational, emotional, dependent, and private; closer to nature than to culture", compared to men and masculinity, who are defined as "rational, scientific, independent, public, and cultured" (McDowell 11), and pointed out that the belief that women are inferior to men is embedded in the structures and practices of Western thought. According to Zuzanna Jakubowski, "conventional discourse originating in the nineteenth century" has imposed "the opposite of masculine characteristics" (22) on women.

Similarly, McDowell claims that gender relations are a "central concern for geographers because of the way in which a spatial division—that between the public and the private, between inside and outside—plays such a central role in the social construction of gender divisions" (12). The extensive attention placed by these geographers on the discourses pertaining to gender divisions originating in the nineteenth century and even in the twentieth century motivated me to examine the gendered space in the Victorian era. According to Daphne Spain, feminist geographers claim that "definitions of femininity and masculinity are constructed in particular places—most notably the home, workplace, and community—and the reciprocity of these spheres of influence should be acknowledged when analysing the status differences between the sexes" (7). As feminist scholars argue, femininity and masculinity linked to the distribution of space and the right to occupy it have produced the belief that women are inferior to men and that the category of femininity is worthless compared to masculinity. McDowell also argues that "the idea that women have a particular place is the basis not only of the social organisation of a whole range of institutions... but also is an essential feature of Western Enlightenment thought" (12). According to Spain, space is organised to reproduce the gender difference in "power and privilege" (233); furthermore, gendered spaces do not change once shaped, and remain inherent in the relationship between power and space. However, as Judith Butler argues, gender is "a relation among socially constituted subjects" and "a shifting and contextual phenomenon", and therefore, it does not indicate "a substantive being" but only "a relative point of convergence among culturally and historically specific sets of relations" (14). I agree with Judith Butler's argument rather than Spain's. Utilising Butler's theoretical lens clarifies that some persons placed in the traditional norm and assigned space have the possibilities to deviate from them when they acknowledge their vulnerability and instability. According to Doreen Massey, space is "the sphere of the possibility of the existence of multiplicity", is "always under construction", and resonates with "shifts" (24). Utilising these perspectives, this study will trace the deviation from Victorian norms and the shifts in the association with mobility in the various literary spaces of the selected novels.

The culture and humanities scholar Doris Bachmann-Medick elucidates the different kinds of "cultural turns" and points out that the "spatial turn" appeared with the slogan "always spatialize" by Fredric Jameson, an exponent of postmodernism, in the 1990s. Bachmann-Medick argues that "current life-worlds coincide with a period dominated to a greater degree by space, simultaneity, and coexistences than by the categories of time, history, and evolution" (211). According to her, space has recently been regarded as a central new unit of perception and a theoretical concept, where "simultaneity and spatial constellations" (211) are highlighted more than temporal categories of history, evolution, progress and development. She claims that a central element of the spatial turn is not "territorial space as container or vessel" but the categorisation of space as "a social production process encompassing perceptions, utilisations and appropriations; a process closely bound up with the symbolic level of spatial representation" (216). Recognising the intimate relationship between space and social aspects allows us to identify the multitude of spatial metaphors used in our lives and literary analysis that have their origins in geography, such as 'displacement', 'marginalise', 'mobility', 'colonisation', 'mapping', 'border', and 'localisation'. Some of these geographical terms have negative connotations, especially those relating to women's spaces. This study recognises the relationship between gendered space and power distribution based on a performative understanding of the social production of both space and gender. Spaces involve power structures and social differences, such as gender, class, age, race, characteristics of the regions, and religion. However, as Butler and Massey highlight, space with power structure is always constructed by society and therefore has the possibility of change. Using their concepts, this study explores the shift of the space produced through the protagonists' mobility. According to Michel Foucault, a "whole history remains to be written of spaces—which would at the same time be the history of powers—… from the great strategies of geo politics to the little tactics of habitat" (1980; 149). Thus, Foucault explicates the connection between space and power and provides the spatial concept of "heterotopias" or other concealed spaces. According to Foucault, "heterotopias" are real places, which are akin to counter-sites, a kind of effectively enacted utopia that has no real site. This study is indebted to Foucault's spatial concept of "heterotopias" to examine the relationship between the space of the protagonists of the selected novels and the construction of their identities.

1.2. Heterotopia (Michel Foucault)

Michel Foucault was inspired by Gaston Bachelard, the phenomenologist who thought that we do not live in a homogeneous and empty space, and extended this perspective to the external space by arguing that "the space in which we live, which draws us out of ourselves…is also, in itself, a heterogeneous space…we live inside a set of relations that delineates sites which are irreducible to one another and absolutely not superimposable on one another" (1998; 239). He was especially interested in the spaces that are "in relation with all other sites", which "suspect, neutralize, or invert the set of relations that they happen to designate, mirror, or reflect" (1998; 239). Foucault refers to two examples of these spaces; the first are utopias, which are a perfected form set in an unreal place, and the other are heterotopias, space concepts created by Foucault. Foucault describes heterotopias as:

> There are also, probably in every culture, in every civilization, real places—places that do exist and that are formed in the very founding of society—which are something like counter-sites, a kind of effectively enacted utopia in which the real sites, all the other real sites that can be found within the culture, are simultaneously represented, contested, and inverted. Places of this kind are outside of all places, even though it may be possible to indicate their location in reality. Because these places are absolutely different from all the sites that they reflect and speak about, I shall call them, by way of contrast to utopias, heterotopias. (1998; 239)

Foucault presents six principles regarding the possible spaces of heterotopia. The first principle is divided into two categories, 'crisis' and 'deviation'. The 'crisis heterotopia' constitutes privileged, sacred, or forbidden places, such as boarding schools for (male) adolescents in the nineteenth century, military service for young men where they are at the mercy of sexual virility, or honeymoon hotels for young women. However, recognising that these heterotopias of crisis are disappearing today, Foucault argues that they are being replaced by the second category, "the heterotopias of deviation" (1998; 240): the spaces for people whose behaviours deviate from the norm, such as retirement homes for old people, psychiatric hospitals, and prisons. Foucault acknowledges the ambiguity between 'the heterotopia of crisis' and 'the heterotopia of deviation', as seen at a retirement home, where old age is both a crisis and a deviation. The second principle of heterotopias is that the function of a heterotopia, such as a cemetery, can change within society as history unfolds. While cemeteries were placed at the heart of the city, next to the church, until the end of the eighteenth century in Western culture, the individualisation of death and the bourgeois appropriation of the cemetery brought about cemeteries' shift to the suburbs. The third principle is that heterotopias can juxtapose several sites in a single real place, such as the theatre and the cinema, where we can see a whole series of places within the rectangular stage or room. The fourth principle is that heterotopias are most often linked to "slices in time" (1998; 242) and accumulation of time, such as in museums and libraries. The idea of enclosing all times within one place belongs to "our modernity" (1998; 242). However, heterotopias are also linked to the temporal, transitory time, such as the festival and the fairgrounds. The fifth principle is that the heterotopia site is not freely accessible and that the individual has to submit to religious rites and hygienic purification, such as the hammam of the Moslems and Scandinavian saunas. The sixth principle is that a heterotopia's role is to create a space of illusion that exposes every real life or to create other real spaces, such as the Puritan societies in America and the Jesuits colony of Paraguay. Recognising the difficulties and ambiguities of these principles, this study will apply several useful principles of heterotopia contrived by Michel Foucault to analyse the space produced by Brontë and Gaskell.

1.3. Mobility

Ingrid Horrocks recently argued that "work on mobility is now exploring the movements of people and things, the meanings, metaphors, and ideologies attached to mobility over time" and that it is also trying to "develop a new set of analytical tools to the complexity of various mechanisms of movement" (21). Moreover, Horrocks claims that "the new methodologies associated with the 'mobilities paradigm' in the social sciences bring into view a whole new range of human movements as movement", and that it provides a way to examine "what happens to people and things (and feelings) in the spaces in between places" (21) more than the scholarship on travel. The key theorisation of mobility that enabled the development of a new set of analytical methods in the social sciences—the mobility turn—was brought about by Tim Cresswell's *On The Move: Mobility in the Modern Western World* (2006), John Urry's *Mobilities* (2007), and Peter Adey's *Mobility* (2010). John Urry, an English sociologist, posits four meanings of the terms, "mobile" and "mobility"; the first is "something that moves or is capable of movement", the second is "a mob, a rabble or an unruly crowd" that cannot be fixed within boundaries, the third is "upward or downward social mobility" like vertical hierarchy of positions, and the fourth is "geographical movement" (8). According to Horrocks, the assumption that "mobility is central to what it is to be modern" (22) is central to their arguments.

Tim Cresswell presents a magnificent survey of the geography and history of mobility in *On The Move* and contributes to the theorisation of the 'mobility turn'. According to Cresswell, mobility signifies "getting from point A to point B" and involves "displacement—the act of moving between locations" (2). Moreover, suggesting the distinction between mobility and movement, Cresswell thinks of mobility as "the dynamic equivalent of place" (3), which signifies "meaningful segments of space—locations imbued with meaning and power" (2), as opposed to movement. Mobility is like space, the central human experience in the world. Thus, Cresswell regards mobility as socially produced motion. When "ideas about mobility" are "conveyed through...representational strategies ranging from literature to philosophy", mobility involves ideological meanings and becomes "synonymous with freedom, with transgression, with creativity, with life itself" (Cresswell 3). Indeed, mobility is how we live, practise, and experience our society, and human mobility is an irreducibly embodied and practised experience as a "part of the process of the social production of time and space" (Cresswell 5). A close reading of the mobilities of mobile protagonists and characters will enable us to trace their practised and embodied experiences, and their sensibility and intellect in the literal space. Cresswell also points out that mobility has a chaotic nature: that is, the stories about mobility are "frequently ideological", for example, the possibility to "connect blood cells to street patterns, reproduction to space travel" (6). The meaning attributed to mobility is rarely just about getting from A to B but also represents significant and "meaningful and laden with power" (Cresswell 9) connotations. Thus, this new way of investigating mobility provided by 'the mobility turn' has contributed to the exploration of literature with abstract, metaphorical, or emotional contents.

Creswell argues that it is remarkable that Thomas Hobbs described "a liberal conception of human mobility—as an individual form of freedom" (14) for the first time in his famous *Leviathan* (1651). However, such an idea of mobility regarded as liberty and freedom did not permeate feudal society, and John Urry claimed that it was not until the eighteenth century that walking was introduced as a means of leisure for men. According to Horrocks, this "privilege" (23) of enjoying walking leisure was accessible only to middle-class men, not women. Similarly, the grand tour and the voyage across the continent of Europe were popular amongst wealthy young men. Horrocks ascribes women's reluctant wandering around the late eighteenth and nineteenth century to their sensibility regarding being excluded from society. As Linda McDowell argues, it was taken for granted for a long time that women's places were in the home. Anne D Wallace argues that regarding walking from the late eighteenth into the nineteenth century, "sexual content" seems to reveal "fearful reactions to women's walking" while "favourable interpretations of men's walking have become standard, not only in literary texts but in experience" (30). My interest in walking as mobility can be ascribed to the conception of walking as the basic form of movement of humans through which they produce space around them. Walking in literary space offers insights into the various issues of gender, religion, class, and region, and the financial, physical, and corporeal information of the characters. Analysing walks by the mobile protagonists in the selected novels is essential to trace their experienced and embodied space within a modernising society. Although walking might be regarded as a form of pre-modern mobility, I would like to demonstrate the interrelation between walking and modernity. The late eighteenth and nineteenth centuries in England and Europe are a remarkable epoch with regards to developments in transport-related technologies. The technology of the construction of roads made great progress, the design of coaches and stagecoaches improved, the roads became safer and more comfortable to travel, and the time taken for journeys by road was shortened. In *Villette* by Charlotte Brontë, the elderly Lucy describes, in retrospect, the distance from the middle of England to London: "[f]ifty miles were then a day's journey" (45). By utilising the expression 'then', the writer seeks to illustrate the shift in the speed of the stagecoach over the preceding decades to the readers. According to Charlotte Mathieson, the expanding road networks in Britain fostered "a sense of national community" (4) and led to an increase in the mobile population who moved from the rural to the urban areas; additionally, travelling for pleasure became popular amongst the mobile middle-classes, including women, and domestic travel for health emerged with the appearance of spa towns and seaside resorts. As Cresswell argues, "the word 'modern' seems to evoke images of technological mobility" (15). In England, the first railway line powered by steam locomotive opened in 1825 between Stockton and Darlington, and the Liverpool to Manchester line was built in 1830. The subsequent railway boom led to the construction of 7500 miles of railway lines in Great Britain by 1852 (Bagwell 93). The advent of the railway contributed to the transportation of people, as well as industrial goods and raw materials. The advancements in the railway networks increased the mobility of not only middle-class people pursuing pleasure and leisure but also working-class people moving from rural to urban areas in pursuit of work. Such revolutions in transportation offer people the opportunity for a changed production of space and new experiences of mobility. The railway became central to capitalist modernity and aided in the development of Great Britain's economy on both a national and global scale. Marshall Berman, a Marxist philosopher, describes capitalist modernity as: "[m]odern environments and experiences cut across all boundaries of geography and ethnicity, of class and nationality, of religion and ideology: in this sense, modernity can be said to unite all mankind" (15). While he admits the benefits of modernity, he remains suspicious that "it is a paradoxical unity, a unity of disunity; it pours us all into a maelstrom of perpetual disintegration and renewal, of struggle and contradiction, of ambiguity and anguish" (15). Berman claims that "to be modern is to be part of a universe in which, as Marx said, 'all that is solid melts into air'" (15). As Berman argues, modernity is not solid nor stable, but ambiguous, mobile, fluid, and unsettled. Similarly, Creswell argues, "modernity is not the enemy of mobility but its friend" (18). People in the Victorian age witnessed the transport revolution, industrial improvement, and territorial expansion based on imperialism, and experienced modernity, which is chaos, flux, and drastic changes. As Anthony Giddens highlights, in the circumstances of modernity "self and society are interrelated" (32). Based on these recent scholars' perceptions, I think that the relation among the protagonists' space, modernity, and their identity is interactive and causative. By deliberately examining the female protagonists' experiences with various forms of mobility, this study will investigate how they build their space and identity in the settings towards modernity.

CHAPTER 2
Walking and Mobility

Charlotte Mathieson makes the following claim about walking: "although walking is the most basic form of mobility, it is also the most physically involved: the limbs are put to work, the body's strength is drawn upon, and every step brings the traveller into contact with the space around them" (19). I consider walking a significant and necessary literary setting within *Jane Eyre* and *Villette* by Charlotte Brontë and *North and South* by Elizabeth Gaskell due to the interconnections between the mobility of the heroines' body and the space around them. The processes of walking serve to develop the character's physical and mental space, as well as advance the development of the narrative. While the Victorian age in Britain saw the construction of the railway network as part of industrialisation, "walking becomes a popular leisure practice among the upper classes" (20) for the first time in this period, according to Mathieson. As she suggests, they appreciate that walking provides them with "freedom, independence, communication with nature, and space for philosophical reflection and creative thought" (20). Generally, however, walking is associated with negative connotations, such as poverty, which the novelists refer to in their works. For example, Nicholas Higgins, a working-class man in *North and South*, walks around the town in his muddy shoes seeking a new job. In the same novel, Margaret Hale explains to Henry Lennox that her father walks to the very extremity of his parish as they have no horse. Thus, walking serves as an indicator of social status and financial circumstances in the narratives. As Mrs Show, Margaret's aunt, does not allow her daughter Edith and Margaret to walk along the street without a footman, walking has a relationship with the issue of gendered politics. In this chapter, I examine how the protagonists produce space around them through walking, either voluntarily or reluctantly, and how their mobilities connect with modernity.

This chapter also examines women's travel by stagecoach, carriage, train, and ship. The middle decades of the nineteenth century witnessed the bristling of railways in large urban and industrial areas and the coach system creating a local communication network by connecting inns, crossing points, relays, and halts. Journey by sea also witnessed dramatic advancements and contributed to making this period one where people no longer lived in one place their whole lives. This chapter will examine how these modern technologies enabled women to undertake long-distance travels. Additionally, it will explore how their bodies experienced and perceived the landscapes they traversed and how they located and dislocated within the places where they belonged.

2.1. *Jane Eyre*
2.1.1. Walking

As Sandra Gilbert and Susan Gubar assert, Jane's "pilgrim's progress toward maturity" (339) is depicted in *Jane Eyre* as she travels "from one significantly named place to another" (342). However, the child Jane is not an active character, and the narrative begins with the sentence "there was no possibility of taking a walk that day", which is subsequently followed by "I never liked long walks, especially on chilly afternoons" (*JE* 9). At Gateshead Hall, while Mrs Reed, Jane's aunt, and her children gather in the drawing room beside a warm fire, Jane retreats to the small breakfast room next to the drawing room and climbs into the window-seat drawn by a red moreen curtain. In this "double retirement", Jane reads Bewick's book, expecting the panes of glass to "protect[ing], but not separate[ing] me from the drear November day" (*JE* 10). Thus, *Jane Eyre* begins with a description of the child Jane's concerns about the bad weather and her physical weakness. Child Jane acknowledges her "physical inferiority" (*JE* 9) —her body's lack of resilience in stepping outside, as her fingers and toes would be nipped in the raw twilight. Thus, the beginning of the novel reveals child Jane's frailty that prevents her from enjoying walks.

At the age of ten, Jane is sent to Lowood School, where poor middle-class daughters are trained to conform to their position and prospects. Every Sunday during the winter season, all the girls have to walk on "an exposed and hilly road", trembling with "bitter winter wind, blowing over a range of snowy summits to the north" (*JE* 72), a two miles journey from Lowood Institution to Brocklebridge Church, which is officiated by their patron, Mr Brocklehurst, to take part in the morning and afternoon service. They are encouraged to march forward "like stalwart soldiers" by following the precept and example of Miss Temple, who is leading them clad in a plaid cloak, "lightly and rapidly along our drooping line" (*JE* 72). The child Jane recognises the contrast between the girls' dispirited walking along the snowy road and Miss Temple's vigorous walking. While Miss Temple's cloak cuts off the frosty wind, the girls' chilblained feet without boots suffer from inflammation so hard that they cannot walk lightly. The girls' chronic sense of hunger from a scanty supply of food also spoils their walking. Although Miss Temple is an affectionate teacher who shows kindness to Jane and her closest friend Helen Burns, as if she were their mother, her behaviour of treating her students like soldiers is bound by the logic of order and discipline. Jane recognises that Miss Temple has "a controlling sense of awe" (*JE* 86) and is ruled by Brocklehurst's authority. According to Michel Foucault, "the development and generalization of disciplinary mechanisms constituted the other, dark side of these processes" (1977; 222). That is, "the representative régime" (Foucault 1977; 222), which includes social institutions such as prisons and schools, functions effectively through disciplinary mechanisms. Poor girls in Lowood Institution are disciplined and controlled through constant and careful surveillance and encouragement. Conceiving that Lowood provides her with "a disciplined and subdued character" (*JE* 100), Jane loses her rebellious spirit from Gateshead, only to endure walking with her frail limbs.

Ironically, it is not until more than half of the girls at Lowood become sick with typhus in spring that Jane enjoys rambling freely. The institution, surrounded by hills and woods, and rising from the verge of a stream, becomes "the cradle of fog-bred pestilence" (*JE* 91). As most teachers' attention is absorbed by the patients, the classes are broken up, regulations are loosened, and "the Orphan Asylum" is transformed into "a hospital" (*JE* 91). The rest of the healthy students, including Jane, gain the opportunity to spend everyday life without the surveillance, rules, and restraints imposed by the teachers and go out of the institution to enjoy themselves freely "in the wood, like gipsies, from morning till night" (*JE* 91). The novel depicts the contrast between the gloomy atmosphere of the sickrooms filled with hospital smells and the fear of death and the pleasant scenery of the outdoors in bright May. The orphan asylum transformed into a hospital on account of the infectious disease is isolated "within its walls" (*JE* 91), buries some dead pupils secretly and deviates from society. Following Foucault's concept of space, Lowood Institution becomes a heterotopic space, which is isolated from the society, "outside of all spaces" (Foucault 1998; 239), where the girls face a "crisis" of infection, and some vigorous girls like Jane develop a "deviant" behaviour against "the required norm" (240). The child Jane would often walk to the nearby wood with her friend, rambles all day long and wades through the stream barefoot to get to her favourite sitting stone. She dines on a piece of cold pie on the broad stone as if it were a sumptuous dinner and enjoys a form of freedom, which she had never previously experienced. Thus, at Lowood Institution, which is transformed into a heterotopic space, Jane is released from the rules, restrictions, and orders of society; this leads to her realising her freedom and innate vigour. However, after losing herself in the wood, Jane notices that the sickness afflicting Helen will rob her of her life.

Consequently, Jane feels "the present" surrounded by an "unfathomed gulf", "formless cloud", "vacant depth", and herself "amid that chaos" (*JE* 94) for the first time. It is the first time when Jane is conscious of life and death. On that particular day, when she happens to lose her way to Lowood Institution, she finds Helen dying. Jane's losing her way in the wood foreshadows her question to Helen regarding where Heaven is. While religious Helen believes in Heaven, Jane is sceptical about the idea. While Jane is engaged in walking, the vital form of human movement, Helen, who has contracted consumption, is confined to the crib in Miss Temple's room. Thus, a contrast is drawn between Jane's energetic mobility outdoors and Helen's static condition indoors. Finding Helen lying in Miss Temple's room, Jane lies beside her and hears her whisper that 'by dying young, I shall escape great suffering'

(*JE* 97). As Gilbert and Gubar argue, Helen "presents a different but equally impossible ideal to Jane" (345) of "self-renunciation, of all-consuming (and consumptive) spirituality" (346). Jane's loss of Helen immediately after her wandering is a narrative strategy employed by Brontë to contrast poor Helen's journey towards death with Jane's journey, motivated by her adventurous spirit, towards development as an independent human being.

Although Jane later becomes a teacher at Lowood on account of Miss Temple's instruction, eighteen-year-old Jane, after seeing off Miss Temple, who resigns from Lowood to get married, realises "the stirring of old emotions" (*JE* 101) and feels that confinement within the walls is no more. She remembers the exciting feeling she experienced when she rambled without restriction in the woods in her childhood. While she looks out of the window at "the blue peaks", she finds that "it was those I longed to surmount; all within their boundary of rock and heath seemed prison-ground, exile limits" (*JE* 101). Tracing the never-ending road, Jane is determined to leave Lowood, the institution of "rules and systems" (*JE* 101). Her opening the window to look out over the landscape and the remote roads signifies her desire to travel the roads and see the world unknown to her. Thus, she is eager to act to induce "change and stimulus" (*JE* 102) in her life; therefore, it can be said that she has a nature of mobility. There is another scene where she goes up to the high place to open the trapdoor and look out at the land surrounding Thornfield, the manor house of Edward Rochester. Finding the life of a governess at Thornfield tedious, Jane often climbs the three staircases to the attic and raises the trapdoor to look out over the landscape. Looking over the fields, hills, and the dim sky-line, she longs for "a power of vision which might overpass that limit; which might reach the busy world, towns, regions full of life I had heard of but never seen; that then I desired more of practical experience than I possessed" (*JE* 129). Her curiosity and desire to go to see the unfamiliar world serve as a reminder that she is designed for mobility. Walking backwards and forwards along the corridor of the third storey makes her soul feel a sense of relief despite her suspicion about Grace's odd murmur. Compared to Margaret Hale's walking in the room motivated by uneasiness and anxiety, as explained later, Jane's walks within the building seem to arise from her strong desire for a new stimulation. She finds her walking along the corridor of the third storey as "the exultant movement" (*JE* 129). She affirms that "human beings oughtn't to be satisfied with tranquillity: they must have action" (*JE* 129). According to Marshall Berman, "to be modern is to find ourselves in an environment that promises us adventure…joy… transformation of ourselves and the world" (15), and so, in this respect, Jane's desire for adventure and action signifies that she has the capacity to live in modernity.

Jane's volunteering to walk to post Mrs Fairfax's letter leads to her first meeting with Rochester. While she has to walk two miles to the post office at Hay, this represents that Thornfield does not exist outside of modernity, represented by the postal network. According to Charlotte Mathieson, "as a major user of the road network, the Post Office was instrumental in aiding road improvements…from the late-eighteenth century" (4). While taking a scenic walk about one mile from Thornfield by herself on a winter afternoon, Jane rests on the stile. Upon seeing a big dog like "the Gytrash", a North-of-England legend, pass her by, she encounters an accident in which the rider and his horse had slipped on the icy road and fallen down. Being in the mood to be helpful, or at least officious, and discovering that there was no one else to help him,

Jane dares to approach the rider and offers him her help. According to Mathieson, "when women do walk, they negotiate a set of gendered codes that operate irrespective of their classed status" (30). However, at this moment, Jane explains to us that she feels no fear of him, only a little shyness. Finding that she does not have an umbrella that can function as a stick, the man, who has twisted his ankle, admits that her help is necessary. He lays his hand on her shoulder, leans on her, and approaches his horse. According to Gilbert and Gubar, Rochester, assuming that she cast a spell upon his horse to make it fall, "acknowledges her powers just as much as (if not more than) her vision of the Gytrash acknowledged his (powers)" (352). As Jane and Rochester have a similar illusion at the same time, they share a similar character. Thus, their relationship begins on the footing of "spiritual equals" (Gilbert and Gubar 352) despite their relationship as master and servant. Furthermore, I think that Rochester's action of leaning on Jane's shoulder is remarkable since it connotes and foreshadows that of blind Rochester in Ferndean in the last scene of the novel, where "he stretched his hand out to be led. I took that dear hand—then let it pass round my shoulder:—I served both for his prop and guide" (*JE* 516). Thus, Jane's first meeting with Rochester while walking by herself to the post office serves as a significant metaphorical scene for the narrative, and it alludes that her vigorous walk contrasted with that of his maimed fragility might reverse their positions within the gendered power structure.

Jane's walking in the orchard of Thornfield in a storm on the evening before her wedding to Rochester is highlighted, in contrast to Rochester's going out on business. He goes out on horseback to his estate of farms thirty miles away as his usual work, leaving her alone at Thornfield Hall. Despite the stormy and strong wind, Jane goes out to walk in the orchard where Rochester would often smoke and which is linked to him. While Jane seems to be confined there even during his absence, she finds a kind of pleasure rather than fear in the wild wind:

> It was not without a certain wild pleasure I ran before the wind, delivering my trouble of mind to the measureless air-torrent thundering through space. Descending the laurel walk, I faced the wreck of the chestnut-tree; it stood up, black and riven: the trunk, split down the centre, gasped ghastly. The cloven halves were not broken from each other, for the firm base and strong roots kept them unsundered below. (*JE* 318)

Her act of running before the violent wind that helps her relieve her troubled mind through space reflects her characteristics of mobility, and her feelings of restlessness and anxiety. The old lightning-struck chestnut tree at Thornfield, which is split down the centre, suggests the image of the future relationship between Jane and Rochester. When Jane talks to the chestnut tree, "the time of pleasure and love is over with you: but you are not desolate: each of you has a comrade to sympathise with him in his decay" (*JE* 319), she considers her wedding with Rochester troublesome despite their comradery. However, in the latter part of the novel, when Rochester, being blind and crippled, compares himself to this old lightning-struck chestnut tree, Jane, free from anxiety, denies this comparison and encourages him by saying that he is like a green and vigorous tree surrounded by plants. Her walk back to the hall through the orchard while gathering apples that had fallen on the ground reveals her feelings of restlessness and anxiety. Her ascertaining whether the fire in the hearth at the library is lit or not before Rochester's return signifies not only her command over domesticity but also the fact that her status will soon be elevated due to being his wife. According to Thad Logan, "the hearth had for Victorians a practical and symbolic centrality in the home" (113). Thus, in contrast to her reckless walk in the stormy rain, she reveals domestic propriety as a middle-class woman who acknowledges the significance of "a cheerful hearth" (*JE* 319).

Jane's discovery that Rochester is secretly hiding his mad wife in the attic compels her to leave Thornfield Hall. In her secret departure, she only takes her purse containing twenty shillings, a straw bonnet and her shawl, leaving Rochester's gifts behind. The dawn before her honeymoon trip to Europe, she has to overcome the temptation to accept the temporary haven given to her by Rochester. Thinking of "drear flight and homeless wandering" (*JE* 369) and expecting that she will have to walk far, she eats some bread and water in the kitchen before departing from her house. Not knowing her destination, she instinctively recognises that she has to go as far as she can, never to return:

> A mile off, beyond the fields, lay a road which stretched in the contrary direction to Millcote; a road I had never travelled but often noticed, and wondered where it led: thither I bent my steps. No reflection was to be allowed now: not one glance was to be cast back; not even one forward. Not one thought was given either to the past, or the future. (*JE* 369)

According to Carol Senf, this brief transitional period is "pivotal" as "she is taking a new direction—not as a wife or mistress or even a schoolgirl or teacher, but as herself" (147). Jane is often depicted as looking out over the distant road from the third floor, and longing for the world which was unfamiliar to her. In this pivotal moment, she is determined to walk in the opposite direction to Millcote, the commerce and merchant town where Rochester had bought her many precious presents following their engagement. Jane's decision to avoid the large manufacturing city reveals that she is determined not to be involved in its seductions and temptations, as pointed out by Henri Lefebvre: "the street in the big city offers… 'seductions', 'temptations'" (Elden, Lebas and Kofman 90). Remarkably, her departure depends on her decision to live as a nobody. Jane skirts fields, hedges, and lanes till after sunrise, walking quickly along her solitary way. Soon, however, "a weakness, beginning inwardly, extending to the limbs" seises her, and she falls, "lying on the ground some minutes, pressing her face to the wet turf" (*JE* 370). Although she fears or hopes that she might die there, she is up "crawling forwards on her hands and knees, and raises to her feet" (*JE* 370). While her movement seems more akin to that of an animal than a civilised woman, it reveals her eagerness to live and determination to overcome hardships. The appearance of a coach gives her a temporary relief, and after two days, paying all her money as a transportation fee, she reaches Whitcross, where a stone pillar is set up at a crossroads where four roads meet. From the well-known names of towns inscribed in the arms of the pillar, she learns that she is presently in a north-midland shire. It is a deserted place, with moorland stretching in all directions; however, it matches Jane's purpose as she does not wish to be seen by anyone. She wonders what she is doing and questions herself:

> Not a tie holds me to human society at this moment—not a charm or hope calls me where my fellow-creatures are—none that saw me would have a kind thought or a good wish for me. I have no relative

but the universal mother, Nature: I will seek her breast and ask repose. (*JE* 371)

According to Mathieson, "Jane may have started her journey on the vehicle (stagecoach) of connection, but having been set down from the network she is now an outcast of the nation with not a tie to bind her" (49). Indeed, Jane is set down by the coach in the moorland as an outcast from the human community and walks alone as a nobody without any destination or anybody's help. She seeks relief and repose in nature, the universal mother. It is natural that Jane considers nature her mother as she is an orphan. According to Linda McDowell, in the history of Western Enlightenment thought, "women are seen as closer to nature... because they menstruate and because of their ability to bear children" (44). Brontë seems to use mother nature as a personification of nature as a woman by stressing its association with fertility and as a force that controls the weather and all living things. However, as McDowell claims, considering nature as female depends on the traditional dichotomy of gender. Jane's traversing of the countryside to reaffirm her connection to nature represents that she is affected by conventional values and that she seeks to connect with a natural power beyond the human being. She walks straight into the heath, finds a moss-blackened granite crag, and sits down under it to feel nature by touching the heath, which is dry and warm from the summer day's heat. Her walking in the moorland is reminiscent of her inclination towards nature as a child, when she used to ramble from Lowood school to her favourite seat, a broad stone in the wood. The sky is pure, a star twinkles kindly, and no breeze whispers. She feels restful and comfortable in the surrounding natural landscape, and clings to nature; "Nature seemed to me benign and good; I thought she loved me, outcast as I was; and I, who from man could anticipate only mistrust, rejection, insult, clung to her with filial fondness" (*JE* 372). The troubles of human society make her cling to nature and feel assimilated with it as "a low mossy swell was my pillow" (*JE* 373); however, her inward anxiety about Rochester prevents her from falling asleep. Becoming aware of her desire for food, she realises that nature does not satisfy all the wants of human beings. Henri Lefebvre claims that although "nature appears as the vast territory of the births", nature is "violent, generous... bountiful, and above all open" (70). While it offers Jane temporal consolation, it does not release her from the suffering from hunger and physical pain. As Lefebvre argues that "nature's space is not staged" (70), its being only exists, even if Jane touches the heath and is moved by its warmth, it does not know why it is so. I suggest that nature does not answer human beings' questions and desire. Finding that she cannot exclusively depend on the blessing of nature, Jane returns to Whitcross and seeks a place where people live and soon begins to walk to a hamlet, whose church bell tells her that "human life and labour [are] near" (*JE* 374). Some pieces of bread in the window at a shop tempt her; however, her offer to exchange her handkerchief for a piece of bread is rejected. She continues to pay attention to the physical suffering caused by hunger and pain in her limbs: "much exhausted, and suffering greatly now for want of food, I turned aside into a lane and sat under the hedge" (*JE* 376). She visits a stranger's house for work as if she were a beggar. Her hunger undermines her pride when she begs a farmer, who is eating his supper, for a piece of bread and eats it when she is out of sight of his house. According to Tamar Heller and Patricia Moran, for the Victorians, "a robust appetite in women" was "a sign of low-class status" or "a sign of moral degradation" (47). The patriarchy subjected women to "womanly morality with delicate health", and therefore, "good women of the upper classes tighten[ed] their corsets and limited their appetites" (Heller and Moran 47). Nevertheless, Brontë persists in describing Jane's starvation through the episode of her long roaming. Her weak limbs are also highlighted from the beginning of her wandering through sentences, such as "my weary, trembling limbs" (*JE* 372), "the apathy that clogged heart and limbs" (374), and "dragged my exhausted limbs slowly" (380). After another uncomfortable night on the damp ground, Jane begs a girl for a bowl of porridge that she was about to throw into a pig trough. Jane's animal-like ravenous devouring of the porridge is far from dignified, and her "wandering about like a lost and starving dog" (*JE* 377) symbolises the "wanderings of the poor orphan child, which constitute her entire life's pilgrimage" (Gilbert and Gubar 363), as stated by Gilbert and Gubar. Bessie used to sing the following for the child Jane; "my feet they are sore, and my limbs they are weary; Long is the way…. Why did they send me so far and so lonely…. Men are hard-hearted, and kind-angels only watch o'er the steps of a poor orphan child" (*JE* 27). As Bessie's song about a poor orphan prophesied, people treat Jane, who asks for food, with suspicion and adopts a distant manner towards her. Jane's reference that "I blamed none of those who repulsed me. I felt it was what was to be expected and what could not be helped" (*JE* 378) reveals that she has reflected on her reckless movement as a woman of nameless and placeless status in a patriarchal society. According to Mathieson, "mobility is situated as a transgressive act for women, and their movement off the beaten track reveals that there is no space for women in the nation's mobile networks" (55). However, throughout her roaming about in the hamlet and the moorland, her body is centred in her space. She experiences the pains of weak limbs and terrible starvation through her process of walking. Giving up struggling to "retain a valueless life" (*JE* 379), Jane leaves the hamlet and walks to the hill through the rain seeking a place to die in. Accidentally discovering the light of Moor House in the distance, she instinctively regards it as her "forlorn hope" (*JE* 380) and drags her exhausted limbs slowly to the house, falling twice, nevertheless, she rises and rallies her faculties to cross the marsh and approach Moor House, the abode of the Rivers family. Her final walk to Marsh End reveals her desperate struggle to live, and her peeping into the room where the Rivers sisters are talking with each other signifies the recuperation of her interest in human society. Her being invited into the house by St John brings "her back into the fold of the national community and back onto the locatable national map" (Mathieson 54). Thus, while several critics consider women's wanderings as being unaccepted by society, it is said that Jane's perambulations while conversing with her body leads her to Marsh End, her ideal domestic space. Tim Cresswell argues that walking is "worthy of several long entries": it provides the entry to "open[ed] up a whole new experience" (212). Indeed, walking leads Jane to the threshold of Moor House, which provides her with new experiences and realisations, thus becoming a long entry into her new space. Thus, Jane's decision to go in the opposite direction of Millcote, six miles from Thornfield, the modern and manufacturing town, which has a silk warehouse and a jeweller's shop from where Mr Rochester bought Jane lots of expensive gifts, opens up a new space for her, neighbouring the small hamlet surrounded by the moor and remote from modernity.

 Jane's walk operates positively or negatively as the space of a woman. Brontë contrives the relationship between women's walking and space as a narrative space of possibility. A woman's roaming was considered to be taboo in the Victorian age; therefore, the description of Jane's wandering was Brontë's attempt to challenge the patriarchal society. Irrespective of how hard and disgraceful her walk is, Jane signifies that she does not yield to hardship. Whenever she falls, she rises again to walk despite the pain in her limbs. This tenacity to live is connected with her desire for food to satisfy her hunger with no regard for her appearance. Brontë insists that our lives experience not only whitewashing but also indecent things, and that even a woman of innocence and pride like Jane stoops down to be a beggar. We have to remember that the name of the place is Whitcross, where a stone pillar is "whitewashed to be more obvious at a distance and in darkness" (*JE* 371). The name of Whitcross, which alludes to "whitewash" —deception or "an attempt to hide unpleasant fact about somebody/something" ("Whitewash", Oxford Learner's Dictionary, def. 2), also refers to St John's hidden nature, selfish nobleness and fastidiousness, as well as the kindness of John Rivers in rescuing Jane from death. Jane's walking serves to extend her opportunities for connections and to produce space. Stemming from her innate curiosity and courage to sustain herself, her walking leads her to her ideal home, the rustic dwelling of the Rivers, where she regains her identity as a middle-class lady before returning to Rochester's adobe.

2.1.2. Travel by Coach and Stagecoach

According to Ruth Livesay, while *Jane Eyre* was published in 1847, when the railways had just begun to displace older modes of transport, such as the stagecoach, this work "looks to the stagecoach era of the 1820s in its carefully just-historical setting" (156). Indeed, the narrative seems to develop in pre-industrial modes. Ten-year-old Jane, who has to go to Lowood by herself, waits for the coach leaving at six at the drive of Gateshead in the morning; "but a few minutes of six, and shortly after that hour had struck, the distant roll of wheels announced the coming coach" (JE 50). By this description, we see that the coach with four horses in those days arrived relatively punctually, and that it served to separate Jane from Bessie, whose neck she clung to until the intervention of the coachman and the guard. Adult Jane describes: "Thus was I severed from Bessie and Gateshead: thus whirled away to unknown, and as I then deemed, remote and mysterious regions" (JE 50). The coach is not depicted as an idyllic mode of transport, but rather as a ruthless one. According to Livesey, judging from the guard's reply, this coach is suggested to be "a mail coach" (169). Jane feels as though the journey to Lowood, covering fifty miles, took as long as that of hundreds of miles; however, she remembers little of the travel except for the coaching inn, where passengers stopped to dine. At this time, having no appetite, the child Jane walks about in the immense room of the inn while fearing that a kidnapper might appear, a thought fuelled by her paranoia. Throughout the novel, Brontë uses the inn to give a little information to the protagonist during the travel of stagecoach. Upon arriving at Lowood in the evening after a long journey in the coach, Jane finds her body to be stiff and is bewildered due to "the noise and motion of the coach" (JE 51). Indeed, her movement by coach from Gateshead to Lowood appears to be an uncomfortable dislocation, which represents that the design of the stagecoach had not been improved yet and that the roads were not smooth prior to the industrial development of modernity. Moreover, as Charlotte Mathieson argues, Jane's "journeys serve to enforce a sense of disruption through the spatially disorienting experience, rather than providing a positive space" (46). Such experiences of journeying by coach are followed by adult Jane's travel.

In contrast to her journeys as a child, Jane's movement from Lowood to Thornfield is planned by herself. Eighteen-year-old Jane, being fascinated by the location of Thornfield, which is nearer to London than her present residence, decides to leave the confinement of Lowood school to become a governess. Departing from Bessie, who comes to see her at Lowood, Jane "mounted the vehicle which was to bear me to new duties and a new life in the unknown environs of Millcote" (*JE* 110). Jane's movement from Lowton to Millcote is not depicted, and her description of the George Inn at Millcote begins with the furniture, which are usually seen in the inn, and the mantelpiece by which she is warming her body. However, her journey by stagecoach is again uncomfortable due to "the numbness and chill contracted by sixteen hours' exposure to the rawness of an October day" (*JE* 111). She left Lowton "at four o'clock a.m., and Millcote town clock is now just striking eight" (*JE* 111). Time, distance, and weather are Jane's great concerns affecting her mobility. Her expectation that somebody will come to pick her up at the inn from Thornfield is betrayed, and she becomes nervous; however, she has to wait until somebody appears. The narrator, adult Jane writes:

> It is a very strange sensation to inexperienced youth to feel itself quite alone in the world, cut adrift from every connection, uncertain whether the port to which it is bound can be reached, and prevented by many impediments from returning to that it has quitted. (*JE* 111–12)

Jane compares herself, a solitary young woman, to a ship, which is uncertain whether to moor at a port or return to the place she departed. She experiences the displacement of two places; the port to which she is bound and the port she has left. She has no abode which she can call her home; now that she has left Lowood School, she cannot return and does not intend to. However, as long as no one comes to see her from Thornfield, she is anxious about whether she will have a place to live in. Her sensibility of displacement experienced in this inn is permeated through her journey. Similarly, in *Villette,* Lucy uses a "life-boat" (*V* 261), which lies "in an old, dark boat-house, only putting to sea...in rough weather" (262) as a metaphor for herself. Thus, in Brontë's works, the protagonists are compared to ships or boats, which symbolise their displacement, solitude, and uncertainty. After a waiter finds a servant from Thornfield at the bar, Jane is able to get in a one-horse vehicle, leaning back in "the comfortable though not elegant conveyance" (*JE* 112). After an hour and a half drive covering six miles brings her to Thornfield, she looks out at the landscape from the window and feels that she is in "a different region to Lowood, more populous, less picturesque: more stirring, less romantic" (*JE* 113). Her comfortable ride on a one-horse vehicle stems from her sense of relief that her journey will finish soon; "I was content to be at length so near the end of my journey" (*JE* 112). Remarkably, she would like her journey to end while she seeks adventure.

Jane's experience of Rochester's "new carriage" (*JE* 306) demonstrates a great difference between Jane's thinking and Rochester's about the matter. Misunderstanding Jane's nature, Rochester thinks that Jane wants precious silk and jewellery like the women whom he has been associated with, and tries to buy her those things in Millcote, the commerce and manufacturing town: "the more he bought me, the more my cheek burned with a sense of annoyance and degradation" (*JE* 309). Rochester's materialism is shared by Adele, his French ward, who wants to accompany them to Millcote but is rejected. Jane's negotiation with Rochester allows Adele to get in the car, which has "so much room" (*JE* 306) for Rochester to hand Adele over to Jane as if she were a little dog. According to Mathieson, "owning a carriage" is referenced as "a marker of social position" (22). Thus, owning a big carriage symbolises the owner's wealth. Rochester's rejection of Adele's request to accompany them clarifies that Adele, Jane's pupil, also inhabits the same marginal space that Jane does. While Jane's description of the landscape is simple and common, Rochester's joke about life on the moon and his comparison of her to a fairy are so fantastical that they make her drive uncomfortable.

Jane's third travel by stagecoach from Thornfield to Whitcross brings Jane to the most problematic circumstances. Jane leaves Thornfield, which she used to think of as "my home—my own home" (*JE* 283), to escape from her marriage to Rochester, who has hidden his mad wife, Bertha, in the attic at Thornfield. Falling to the ground outside Thornfield Hall several times, she reaches the road and sits under the hedge until she hears the wheels of the stagecoach. Asking the driver where he was heading, Jane recognises that the destination was a place which Rochester had no connection with and negotiates the fare to get her there; "he said thirty shillings; I answered I had but twenty; well, he would try to make it do" (*JE* 370). However, after two days' drive, she is set down by the coachman at a place called Whitcross on the way to the destination. Whitcross is not a hamlet, only the site of a stone pillar where four moorland roads meet. Jane thinks that the reason the pillar is "whitewashed" is to be "more obvious at a distance and in darkness" (*JE* 171). However, I suggest that the name of the place, "Whitcross", connotes that the coachman sets down Jane at the moorland remote from any village counter to his promise. The whitewashed pillar of "Whitcross" alludes not only to the cheating of the coachman but also to St John's paternal pressure on Jane beneath his fine appearance as a clergyman. Disconnected from the network of stagecoaches and abandoned in the deserted moorland, Jane has to wander while suffering the pain of her limbs and hunger. As Mathieson points out, Jane is severed from human society and "cast out from the network of the nation" (49). Thus, Brontë represents the stagecoach as a mode of transport that leads to Jane's ordeal.

In the last leg of the journey from Whitcross to Thornfield by stagecoach, Jane feels "like the messenger-pigeon flying home" (*JE* 487). The messenger-pigeon is a domestic pigeon that has the ability to find its way home, however far it may be. From the foot of the signpost of Whitcross, she gets in the same stagecoach that had set her down one year previously; however, she is no longer the same person. As she mentions, she is relieved from the anxiety that she is "obliged to part with my whole fortune as the price of its accommodation" (*JE* 487). She knows her destination, has enough money, and articulates the long distance:

> It was a journey of thirty and six hours. I had set out from Whitcross on a Tuesday afternoon, and early on the succeeding Thursday morning the coach stopped to water the horses at a wayside inn, situated in the midst of scenery whose green hedges and large fields and low pastoral hills…met my eye like the lineaments of a once familiar face. (*JE* 487)

Instead of the scenery during the long way, the landscape around the inn attracts her attention on this journey. She feels that she is near Thornfield Hall, whose landscape she is familiar with. Informed that Thornfield Hall was two miles from the inn, whose sign read "The Rochester Arms", Jane decides to walk there instead of going by carriage. For her, neither a stagecoach nor a carriage serves as the means of producing her space, which she feels empathy for. In the last scene, learning that Rochester was living in Ferndean, about thirty miles away from the inn, she heads for the place using a chase, a sort of carriage; however, she alights from the vehicle one mile before the manor-house: "the last mile I performed on foot, having dismissed the chaise and driver with the double remuneration I had promised" (*JE* 496). Jane walks along the narrow path to the house inhabited by Rochester, absorbing the atmosphere of the secluded place. To depict how Jane's emotional excitement is elevated as she approaches her and Rochester's home, Brontë thinks that walking is more suitable than going by coach or any transportation, which brings her protagonist quickly without sufficient observation and appreciation. Both a stagecoach and a coach can only function as a means of transporting her from one place to another, and to clarify the distance and time. In this crucial instance, only walking can satisfy her interest or curiosity, and prepare her for the new developments.

2.2. *Villette*
2.2.1. Walking

As Lucy Morrison argues, "Lucy Snow is a principally peripatetic traveller whose walking enables, facilitates, and even excuses and evokes her psychological reveries" (186–87). This is evident from the very beginning of the novel. It is when she returns "from a long walk" (*V* 6) to Mrs Bretton, her godmother's house that Lucy learns of the arrival of Polly (Paulina Mary Home), the daughter of Mrs Bretton's acquaintance. Fourteen-year-old Lucy used to like the clean and ancient town named Bretton, with "a fine antique street" (*V* 5) and its quiet atmosphere. Thus, the Bretton family lives in the town that bears their family name. In contrast to the opening sentence in *Jane Eyre*, a long walk is the favourite activity of the child Lucy. She explains about her feelings on leaving Bretton, "little thinking then I was never again to visit it; never more to tread its calm old streets" (*V* 35). Walking along the quiet antique streets in Bretton was a source of comfort for the orphaned Lucy. Although young Lucy acquires a job as the live-in companion for Miss Marchmont, her death leads her to lose both her abode and job. Driven into a corner after departing Miss Marchmont's mansion, Lucy consults a housekeeper who was once her nurse and learns that many English women work as nurses in foreign families. Walking two miles from the housekeeper's house in the twilight brings her "the vigour of a youth" (*V* 43) and "some new power" (44), and she hears an inner voice speak to herself: "Leave this wilderness and go out hence" (*V* 44) with the backdrop of the information relating to English nurses abroad. Although "wilderness" is an incongruous expression in contrast to "that flat, rich middle of England" (*V* 44), Lucy considers the country of the middle of England not only as a hopeless and restrained space intertwined with her experiences of living in her relative's or at Miss Marchmont's house, but also as an inanimate and monotonous rural district. In walking along the dim, narrow path, Lucy is urged to go to London by a strong inner feeling; "it was better to go forward than backward, and that I could go forward—that away, however narrow and difficult, would in time open—predominated over other feeling" (*V* 47). Lucy considers the two miles' walk from Miss Marchmont's not to be a long distance, and this walk provides her with vigour, energy and courage to leave the country to build a new life.

Lucy, the narrator, reminisces that driving fifty miles to London by stagecoach took a day in the early nineteenth century. Since the narrator with snowy white hair is old when she describes these events, she provably arrived in London about forty years previously. When she first arrives in London on a rainy night, she feels as if its vastness and strangeness are similar to that of ancient Babylon. Lucy, a twenty-three-year-old woman, who arrives in London from rural middle-England, feels lost in the metropolitan city: "How difficult, how oppressive, how puzzling seemed my flight!" (*V* 46) Looking at St. Paul's Dome from the window of the hotel on the next morning after her arrival, Lucy notices a change within herself: "While I looked, my inner self moved; my spirit shook its always-fettered wings half loose; I had a sudden feeling as if I, who never yet truly lived, were at last about to taste life" (*V* 48). For the first time, Lucy feels that she has been unshackled from the physical and material confinement of the hamlets of middle England and appreciates her newfound freedom; "the spirit of this great London", where "the solemn, orbed mass, dark blue and dim" of the Dome (*V* 48) is the symbol. According to Liana F. Piehler, "the word 'orb' itself seems to connote entities beyond the architectural, perhaps even to cosmic proportions" (46). Indeed, fascinated by the orbed mass of the Dome, she mounts it to peer over London.

Consequently, she recognises the wideness of the surrounding world and decides to not only keep her project in London but later cross the sea to travel to the continent; that is, she comes to recognise her place within the cosmic scale. As Marshall Berman argues that experiences of space and time in modern circumstances make us go beyond the geographical boundaries (15), Lucy broadens her world from rural confinement to the modern urban circumstances of London. Lucy is reflective of the space she occupies: "Presently I found myself in Paternoster-row.... I mounted to the [St. Paul's] dome... I saw antique Westminster... Temple Garden" (*V* 49). Lucy, who was displaced in the middle of England, seems to find her place in London, and appears to be comfortable amidst its traditional architecture and places. Walking alone in London serves as an adventure in itself that provides her with elation and pleasure. The aspect that moves her most is the bustling city life witnessed in the business district:

> I got into the Strand; I went up Cornhill; I mixed with life passing along; I dared the perils of crossings. To do this, and to do it utterly alone, gave me, perhaps an irrational, but a real pleasure.... I have seen the West End... but I love the city far better. The city seems so much more in earnest: its business, its rush, its roar, are such serious things, sights, and sounds. The city is getting its living—the West End but enjoying its pleasure. (*V* 49)

Lucy is more interested in the bustling and busy streets filled with the lives of people than the quiet parks and fine squares. She evaluates the seriousness of the capitalist modernity observed in the city and feels an affinity with the earnest living she observes. Her evaluation of the city seems to stem from her consciousness that she has to earn a living as an orphan. Her consciousness leads to an upheaval of her self-confidence: "who but a coward would pass his whole life in hamlets; and forever abandon his faculties to the eating rust of obscurity?" (*V* 48) Lucy assumes that life without adventure or challenge will be boring. Her walk in London by herself is an adventure in itself; and she describes the experience of crossing the street at the crossing as "utterly alone, gave me, perhaps an irrational, but a real pleasure" (*V* 49). As for these depictions, Lucy Morrison argues:

> She [Lucy] both sees and feels as she mixes with the life moving around her but seems, still, to keep at a distance—she becomes a part of the scene, but her consciousness of making herself a part of the scene simultaneously underscores her separateness from the urgency of lives being led by the flood of people surrounding her" (189).

As Morrison argues, while she is in the flood of the crowd, Lucy feels "utterly alone", but "a real pleasure" and the "ecstasy of freedom and enjoyment" (*V* 49). She enjoys sharing the same time and space with strangers, but at the same time, she is glad that she remains totally alone as her mind yearns to keep a distance from others. Thus, Lucy's walk in the modern city, London, is her private enjoyment; she does not seek a new community or unity. After a walk, she feels hunger, a sense which she had forgotten since her time in Miss Marchmont's house, and delightful fatigue and sleepiness. Thus, her walk in the city also allows her to regain her healthy young body and a positive mind. After the walk, her meditation at the hotel leads her to acknowledge that she has neither home nor person to mourn her even if she were to die in England, and she resolves to move to the continent by sea to secure a job. Two days' stay in London provides Lucy with both the pleasure of walking freely in the city and cognisance regarding her displacement.

Unlike her walks in the urban streets in London, Lucy becomes an unreliable walker in Villette, the foreign city. On arriving at the suburbs of Villette by stagecoach, her confusion at losing her trunk is followed by an English gentleman's kindness in leading her to a nearby hotel. The park is "black as midnight" with "the double gloom of trees and fog" (*V* 63), and the path is miry with the water dripping from the trees. In contrast to her courageous walks alone in London, Lucy follows a gentleman's tread barely, sometimes nearly losing sight of him. As it is a rainy night in the foreign town, her lack of self-confidence in walking becomes highlighted. She strangely relies on the tread of an English gentleman whom she has just met, and later the handsome gentleman proves to be the only son of Mrs Bretton—Dr John. Later, Dr John again becomes a trustful guide for Lucy, which signifies her willingness to rely on somebody else and her hidden affection for him. However, his guidance finishes at the end of the park, and to her disappointment, Lucy loses her way despite his advice and memo written about the hotel's name, becoming fearful of being followed by two mysterious men. Although these men later prove to be the teachers at Madame Beck's school, Lucy is scared that she may be under surveillance in Villette. Thus, Lucy's solitary and uneasy condition in Villette has continued since her arrival at the foreign harbour. After walking for a while, she happens upon the brass plate inscribed with "Pensionnat de Demoiselles" and "Madame Beck" in the door of a rather large house. According to Sandra M. Gilbert and Susan Gubar, "Lucy accidentally finds her way to Madame Beck's house because it is the house of her own self" (408). Indeed, she follows her inner voice, "Stop here; this is your inn" (*V* 64) and rings the doorbell. Though Lucy was left in the strange place by the pursuers, her faculty to manage to search for her destination leads her to her own place even in the darkness at night. As Lucy's remark "your inn" indicates, Madame Beck's boarding school becomes her place to stay and live in, not her home, but a temporary abode.

Advanced to the position of an English teacher, Lucy finds walking in the school garden at the Rue Fossette both pleasant and valuable, as it is the only place free from Madame Beck's control and surveillance. Madame Beck has a "face of stone", haunts the house and school "as a shadow" (*V* 70) in her "soundless slippers" (71), and manages the establishment under the watchwords, "surveillance" and "espionage" (72). The school garden is the only space free from Madame Beck's control. Lucy must be satisfied with the school garden—the narrow artificial garden in the cosmopolitan city. Although there is a tradition that a young nun was buried alive for some sin at the foot of an old pear tree and that her ghost haunts the area, Lucy enjoys lingering solitarily on summer mornings and evenings in the garden, tasting the evening breeze, straying down the peaceful alleys alone, and hearing the bells of St. Jean Baptiste. Lucy's favourite walking space is "l'allée défendue" (*V* 107), an alley that runs parallel with the very high wall without windows and housing the boys' college's boarding-houses on the other side. Entry to this alley is forbidden to the pupils, and it is seldom entered by the teachers on account of its narrowness, very thick shrubs, and its roof of branches and leaves. However, Lucy confesses that "the seclusion, the very gloom of the walk attracted me" (*V* 108). As the narrow path is characterised by "shades" being "not prominent", and "no more to be parted with than my identity" (*V* 108), she takes care of the path and cleans up the rustic seat. Sitting on the hidden seat, Lucy listens to "what seemed to be the far-off sounds of the city" (*V* 108):

> Far-off, in truth, they were not: this school was in the city's centre; hence, it was but five minutes' walk to the park, scarce ten to buildings of palatial splendour. Quite near the wide streets brightly lit, teeming

at this moment with life: carriages were rolling through them to balls or the opera. The same hour which tolled curfew for our convent, which extinguished each lamp, and dropped the curtain round each couch, rang for the gay city about us the summons to festal enjoyment. Of this contrast I thought not, however. (*V* 108–09)

The streets outside the school premises convey the hustle and bustle of the metropolitan city in the evening. Sitting on the seat in the tranquil school alley by herself, Lucy listens to the noises in the street and turns her thoughts or imaginations to the movements of people seeking entertainment or amusement. Although the contrast between the quiet and regulated life of convents and the free activities of people outside of the girls' dormitory does not make her miserable, she has a "calm desire to look on a new thing" (*V* 109) as an observer in modernity. Thus, Lucy does not want to distance herself from the new or modern things and feels the energy of the cosmopolitan city as she had in London. Confined within the little garden in the centre of the city, she does not envy the persons outside the dormitory as she acknowledges that she does not have gay instincts. However, the incident involving the casket with the love letter being dropped at Lucy's feet, which is followed by Dr John's arrival, disturbs her rest and reveries in the garden.

According to Lucy Morrison, Lucy "no longer feels utterly alone as she did in London: she is not even always solitary but is desirous of refuge and a space of her own beyond the gayest bustle of the interior domestic scene" (190). However, her personal favourite garden and path are intruded on by other people, not only Dr John but also M. Paul, and "their seclusion was now become precarious", and "their calm— insecure" (*V* 116); thus, Lucy loses her secluded, private, and secure space. In the alley, M. Paul, the professor of literature who has observed Lucy's movements from the window facing the alley, offers her his friendship. At the school, Lucy is often annoyed by many complaints from Miss Ginevra Fanshawe, a thriving beautiful pupil supported by rich relatives and has suitors, Le Colonel Alfred and Dr John. According to Gilbert and Gubar, Ginevra embodies "Lucy's attraction to self-indulgence and freedom" (409). I do not agree that Lucy is attracted to self-indulgence, as Lucy is so irritated with Ginevra's selfish words and actions that she drives Ginevra out of her apartment. Another source of annoyance for Lucy is Madame Beck's espionage and surveillance, but Lucy mocks Madame Beck upon catching her search through the drawer of Lucy's toilet. As Diane Long Hoeveler argues that "because Madame is using her eyes in the same way the early Lucy surreptitiously used hers", Madame and Lucy "are doubles for each other" (226). Indeed, Madame Beck walks like a shadow and keeps surveillance of all the teachers similar to Lucy, who is a "looker-on" (*V* 141). As the narrow alley in the garden comes to be intruded on by other teachers, Lucy finds refuge in the interior of the dormitory, her own quarter:

> When I vanished—it was into darkness; candles were not allowed to be carried about, and the teacher who forsook the refectory, had only the unlit hall, schoolroom, or bed room, as a refuge.... In summer it was never quite dark, and then I went up-stairs to my own quarter of the long dormitory, opened my own casement, and leaning out, looked forth upon the city beyond the garden, and listened to band-music from the park or the palace-square, thinking meantime my own thoughts, living my own life, in my own still, shadow-world. (*V* 117–18)

Lucy is lost in her thoughts, listening to band music from the city, and by opening the window, she can taste freedom and the open air as if she were in the garden. Although Madame Beck's school and dormitory are enclosed places, Lucy can feel the metropolitan atmosphere and stimulate her imagination in the marginal space of the dormitory. Thus, while Lucy belongs to the public sphere of the school and dormitory, she constantly seeks a private space. Lucy does not gain rest and calm in the school, "a strange, frolicsome, noisy little world" (*V* 127); instead, she tries to escape from the public space and search for her own private space to confine herself within. Lucy's actions present an interesting paradox; she finds the physically constrained space of the dormitory to be a public space that offers her no privacy, and instead, she finds a private space by imagining herself to be in the physically open space of the garden.

Lucy strives to acquire a larger space to feel freedom when Madame Beck and her family, M. Paul, and the other teachers leave the school for a long summer vacation:

> I was free to walk out. At first I lacked courage to venture very far from the Rue Fossette but by degrees I sought the city gates, and passed them, and then went wondering away far along chausses, through fields, beyond cemeteries, Catholic and Protestant, beyond farmsteads, to lanes and little woods, and I know not where. A goad thrust me on, a fever forbade me to rest; a want of companionship maintained in my soul the cravings of a most deadly famine. (*V* 158)

While she is liberated from Madame Beck's surveillance or confinement in the school, Lucy's walks by herself in September do not offer her pleasure but rather lead to self-torment. Her feelings of solitude and great loneliness in the long empty dormitory prompt her to leave the school and walk in the city and beyond. Wandering aimlessly, Lucy only imagines what her acquaintances are doing; Madame Beck is enjoying herself with her children at a watering place, M. Paul is on a pilgrimage in Rome, other teachers have left the city, and Ginevra Fanshawe will be the happiest as she is on tour southward. Through these musings, Brontë lists the new forms of enjoying summer vacation that became popular throughout the early years of the nineteenth century. According to Charlotte Mathieson, visiting the country house, pilgrimages, and spending time in spa towns and seaside resorts became "an enjoyable pursuit for the mobile middle classes" (3). Lucy's walks while imagining her acquaintances' modern pursuits of vacationing torment her, and thus, she cannot endure her state of isolation and misery. Her aspirations and interests undergo a cataclysmic change, and she is no longer fascinated by her free walks beyond the city into the countryside. Her solitude and depression stem from her pessimistic outlook regarding the future and the contrast between her situation and that of her acquaintances or doubles, Madame Beck and Ginevra.

Consequently, her solitary walk in Villette thinking about her acquaintances contrasts with her enjoyable walk in London among foreigners. The contradictory description that Lucy, who needed her private space while the inhabitants were in the dormitory, suffers from isolation as soon as they leave that place signifies that she feels displacement. Indeed, this dilemma leads her to the confessional in the Catholic Church, despite her being a Protestant.

Dr John Bretton rescues Lucy, who is lying outside the church after a long walk in spite of her physical weakness and mental confusion.

During her stay at la Terrasse, Dr Bretton and his mother's home in the suburbs, he offers Lucy both repose and his perfect knowledge of Villette. He takes her to various places of interest in the city that she was unaware of, which covers not only its open streets and the public and modernised places such as galleries, museums, and halls but also the poor and crowded inner-city district of Basse-Ville. Accompanying him to examine his patients, Lucy finds he goes beyond his duty as a doctor, noticing that he is not so much a physician as a philanthropist. Thus, in treating the poor patients in the kingdom of Labassecour with cheerful, habitually kind attitude, he seems to overcome the boundary of class, geography, and nationality, and displays the talent to live in modernity. His energetic and confident walking in the public sphere is in contrast to Lucy's private walk, tormented by the loneliness and uncertainty of the future in a foreign country. She feels admiration for his possessing the "Open! Sesame!" (*V* 198) to expand his sphere of action. Recognising his kindness and benevolence without distinction in the public space, Lucy argues that he is not perfect in the private space, highlighting his human weakness that his passion for Ginevra Fanshawe's beauty makes him blind as well as "his masculine self-love" (*V* 197). Indeed, throughout the narrative, Dr John often appears as a good guide and trustful friend for Lucy and thanks to him, she frequently has a chance to access the wide outer world where she cannot go by herself. However, through their walks, Lucy often acknowledges that he is "not perfect" (*V* 197). The episode in which he appeared as a kind gentleman upon her arrival at Villette and offered to take her halfway to her hotel, but eventually, his insufficient guidance caused her to become lost on the rainy night, demonstrates that he is not the best-qualified person to lead her. She has to discover her own way and destination by herself, or rather, she exemplifies that she has the ability to do so. However, as she regards him as "a cicerone after my own heart" (*V* 198), she prefers walking alone as she likes to be guided perfectly from the beginning to the end.

Lucy considers walking with Ginevra, her beautiful pupil who boasts of her background under M. de Bassompierre's guardianship, troublesome. However, as Gilbert and Gubar argue, there are "resemblances between Ginevra's satiric wit and Lucy's sardonic honesty" (409–10), and only Ginevra is aware of the true nature of Lucy. Asking Lucy who she is, Ginevra suspects Lucy's true character and suggests that Lucy is "anybody", "peculiar and so mysterious" (*V* 309). When Lucy and Ginevra visit Miss de Bassompierre or little Paulina (Polly), the cousin of Ginevra, Ginevra suggests to Lucy that she should take her arm to walk together. Thus, Ginevra recognises that she and Lucy "should now be so much on a level, visiting in the same sphere; having the same connections" (*V* 307). According to Charlotte Mathieson, in *Shirley*, "it is through walking together that Caroline and Shirley's friendship is solidified" (30). Indeed, walking together and having conversations allow the women to develop a friendship between them, and Lucy suggests that they should walk side by side without taking each other's arms. Lucy hates Ginevra's taking her arm and leaning upon Lucy her whole weight. However, Ginevra insists that "offering to take your arm" is meant as "a compliment" (*V* 308). There is a difference between the "estimate" (*V* 309) of Ginevra and Lucy: Ginevra thinks that an attitude of reasonable integrity is a product of birth or wealth and some consciousness of name or connection, but Lucy thinks that the aspect that matters is whether a person's personality is appreciated duly. Ginevra despises Dr John as he belongs to the middle class, unlike her suitor, Colonel de Hamal, who is a count. Lucy makes light of "pedigree, social position, and recondite intellectual acquisition" and "to whom could be assigned only the small sitting-room and the little bedroom: even if the dining and drawing-rooms stood empty" (*V* 309). Thus, she uses the spatial image to underline her view which transgresses the norm of society in those days.

As Lucy Morrison points out, "Lucy physically and mentally needs to walk" (192). Whenever she is "in melancholy moods", she walks "by instinct" (*V* 295) to the old historical quarter of the town in Villette, which has hoaxed and overshadowed precincts. One day, possessed by the thought that she would like to bury the letters from Dr John/Graham Bretton in the garden, she wanders on from street to street to find a kind of broker's shop, where she puts the letters into a glass bottle she had bought and has the bottle stoppered and sealed by the broker. Consequently, she has "a dreary something" and "a sad, lonely satisfaction" (*V* 295). On returning to the school dormitory in the evening, she steals into the allée défendue (forbidden narrow path), walks to the old pear tree near her seat, and finds a deep hollow near its root, hidden by ivy. She thrusts the bottle deep in it, puts the slate, secures it with cement, and buries it. While she confesses that she "was not only going to hide a treasure" but she "meant also to bury a grief" (*V* 296), she decisively determines to bid farewell to her friend, Dr John. While her movement appears transgressive, "lingering like any other mourner" near the grave brings her the feeling of "reinforced strength" (*V* 296). While walking in the allée défendue would often comfort her solitude and provide her with private space, the legend that a young nun was buried in the garden is conflated metaphorically with her action of burying her "treasure" and "grief" in the garden. According to Gilbert and Gubar, the appearance of the nun at the burial in the alley "forecasts the ways in which Dr John will continue to haunt Lucy" (427). However, when Lucy sees the ghost of the nun in this path, Lucy no longer depends on Dr John nor consults him about it, unlike when she saw it for the first time in the attic of the school. This indicates that Lucy has grown apart from Dr John and does not want him to intrude on the secret alley, which is tightly connected and associated with her identity.

Lucy's positive impression of the Basse-Ville proves to have a paradoxical connotation on her next visit. When Madame Beck asks Lucy to deliver a basket filled with fruit to Madame Walravens at Basse-Ville later in the narrative, Lucy's attitude highlights the old and gloomy atmosphere of the ruined town:

> Antiquity brooded above this region, business was banished thence. Rich men had once possessed this quarter, and once grandeur had made her seat here. That church, whose dark, half-ruinous turrets overlooked the square, was the venerable and formerly opulent shrine of the Magi. But wealth and greatness had long since stretched their gilded pinions and fled hence.... As I crossed this deserted place, on whose pavement drops almost as large as a five-franc piece were now slowly darkening, I saw, in its whole expanse, no symptom or evidence of life. (*V* 387)

Walking to the house of Madame Walravens, Lucy thinks over the history of Basse-Ville, the contrast between its former grandeur and wealth supported by flourishing businesses and its current ruinous poverty. According to Carl Plasa, it is "a mirroring of the desuetude into which Madame Walravens' colonial holdings have lapsed" (149). Indeed, Madame Beck's present of "fine hothouse fruit...reposing amongst the dark green, wax-like leaves, and pale yellow stars" of "exotic plant" (*V* 386), whose names Lucy does not know, seems to be suitable for Madame Walravens, who was left a plantation in Guadeloupe, the West Indian state, by her husband. Through the impoverished widow, Brontë represents the circumstances affected by Britain's imperialism in those days and the business or commercial ventures in the colonies. As Plasa argues about the monetary metaphor, "the terms in which Lucy represents the storm's onset suggest the incipient return of past prosperity, as the pavement beneath her feet becomes slowly darkened by drops of rain, each of which is almost as large as a five-franc pierce" (149). To the end of the novel, M. Paul is elected as a "competent agent" (*V* 461) to manage the estate, making it productive and successful in a few years. According to Mathieson, there was a prevailing mood in Britain and Europe, "which conceived of the world as open for imperialist expansion and acquisition" (124) under the globalising effects of capitalist modernity. The people around Lucy in the cosmopolitan city of Europe, Villette, are also involved in the profits and risks of capitalist modernity. Madame Walravens' malice, which Lucy feels in her inhospitable salon, is associated with her exploitative colony and her exploitation of M. Paul's goodness and is represented by evoking a peal of thunder and a flash of lightning when she sees Lucy. Such a sudden storm in Basse-Ville might be a metaphorical indication of the shipwreck that M. Paul will suffer at the end of the novel.

 Realising that Madame Beck is preventing her from seeing M. Paul before his departure to Guadeloupe, Lucy tries to escape from the classes of Rue Fossette. However, Madame Beck gives Lucy a strong opiate to confine her for the night; in this instance, Lucy conceives that the dormitory is "great dreary jails" (*V* 451) and yearns for freedom. The opiate, however, has the effect of inducing excitement in Lucy rather than a stupor. On the hot July night, when the dormitory sleeps soundly, Lucy, wearing a large hat and shawl, opens the huge and heavy portal doors easily as if some dissolving force guided her. Upon leaving the school site, she hears music and is drawn toward the park, where she finds herself plunged among a gay, living, joyous crowd. She sees an open carriage pass her carrying the familiar faces of Mrs Bretton, Dr John, Paulina Mary, and her father, the Count de Bassompierre. Lucy follows them, thinking that none of them recognises her, and realises that following them without being noticed is strangely pleasurable.

Enjoying the role as an onlooker, Lucy goes across the iron gateway into the park and finds herself "in a land of enchantment…a region, not a trees and shadow, but of strangest architectural wealth—of altar and of temple, of pyramid, obelisk, and sphinx…, the wonders and the symbols of Egypt teemed throughout the park of Villette" (*V* 453). Lucy wonders at the change in setting offered by the park compared to the rest of the city, a change from the modern metropolitan city into one filled with the symbols of ancient Egypt. However, soon she recognises that all these artefacts are made of timber as spectacles for the festival. According to Michel Foucault, "festivals" are the "heterotopias", which are "external space" linked to "time in its most flowing, transitory, precarious aspects", and they are "rather absolutely temporal" (1998; 239–42). Indeed, Lucy sees the "marvellous empty sites" with "stands, displays, heteroclite objects" (1998; 242), which Foucault points out. At the same time, Foucault argues that the experiences of a festival are just as much about the rediscovery of "time" (1998; 242). Lucy also traces the history of Labassecour and the origin of the festival, remembering that the festival honours citizens and patriots who have died for their freedom and rights.

Considering that the pyramid, obelisk, and sphinx are symbols of the power and authority of the ancient kings of Egypt, these spectacles do not seem appropriate for the festival but rather seems to represent something contrary. This is why I cannot agree with Liana F. Piehler's argument that "this exotic land of delight has its root in the town of Villette" (59). I would rather argue that such fake spectacles of Egypt are linked with the stratagem designed by Madame Walravens to entrap M. Paul. Madame Walravens is a cruel and greedy woman who objected to M. Paul's marriage with her granddaughter owing to his poverty, thus making her granddaughter kill herself.

Nevertheless, Madame Walravens makes him help her with her living expenses and tries to revive her plantation with his aid. Brontë is always conscious of the global space and geographical power in the Victorian age. She draws attention to the fact that Egypt was under the control of the European powers and that the European countries coveted the historical fortunes of Egypt; furthermore, she draws a parallel between this situation and that in the plantations of Guadeloupe, in the West Indies. At the festival, Lucy sees M. Paul enjoying a conversation with his godchild, surrounded by Madame Beck, Madame Walravens, and the old priest Silas. The topic of their conversation is M. Paul's voyage to Guadeloupe, where he is to manage Madame Walravens' plantation under imperialism. While good-natured Paul does not detect Madame Walravens' group's conspiracy, Lucy is aware that his departure from Europe is to be an "expatriation" (*V* 462). Most inhabitants in the cosmopolitan European city of Villette conceive the pyramid, sphinx, and obelisk as symbols of Egypt in North Africa, and themselves as inhabitants of a world of modernity. While Marshall Berman claims that we break every border and boundary in modern environments, he points out that modernity does not "unite all mankind" (15). I would like to add that Brontë realises this "disunity" (Berman 15) and elucidate the complicated problems of modernity through the novel.

When Lucy decides to leave the festival in the park, she follows the ebb of the people who are returning home:

> These oil-twinkling streets are very still: I like them for their lowliness and peace. Homeward-bound burghers pass me now and then, but these companies are pedestrians, make little noise, and are soon gone. So well do I love Villette under her present aspect. (*V* 469)

Lucy is fond of the quiet streets and the humbleness and peace of Villette. These aspects of Villette resemble those of Bretton, the clean, ancient, and quiet town with a fine street, which the child Lucy loved. According to Ellen Moers, Bretton is "a place between places, neither Continental nor English" (230). In her favourite city—Villette—Lucy walks amongst burghers, who are strangers to her; most of them are quiet pedestrians, who do not bother her. While they sometimes pass her, Lucy does not mix with them as she did in London. As Morrison argues, "they are not, after all, her company...in Villette, she is a part of the scene and consciously displaces herself from its activity into the position of an observer" (192). Akin to the pedestrians in Villette, Lucy can walk at her own pace as she did in London. Accordingly, Lucy places herself in Villette, where she can walk at her own pace and live her life as an observer while keeping her distance from the inhabitants.

While Madame Beck attempts to prevent Lucy from meeting M. Paul directly, Lucy is invited by M. Paul to a walk with him into the town.

Lucy's reliance on him is revealed by her not disregard for ascertaining their destination. During their walk, a long distance along the boulevards, M. Paul is cognisant of her physical fatigue, and his kindness is highlighted in contrast to his severity in the school. This is exemplified by his response to her question of whether or not she displeases his eyes, borne out of her inferiority complex regarding her outward appearance when he lets her rest on the bench. His answer encourages and satisfies her so much that she decides to forget about others' opinions regarding her appearance. By his words, Lucy is liberated from her "fear" about "what she might be for the rest of the world" (*V* 484). Although such fears must have urged her to act like a shadow, Lucy feels confident that M. Paul approves of her appearance. As Diane Long Hoeveler argues, "she is lead to by M. Paul to a proper assessment of herself and her place in the world" (239). Thus, her walk with M. Paul brings her self-confidence and pleasure. When they reach the middle of a clean Faubourg, he stops before the white doorstep of a very neat abode and invites her into the house. She notices M. Paul open the door with the key taken from his pocket and that the small house was freshly painted:

> Opening an inner door, M. Paul disclosed a parlour, or salon—very tiny, but I thought, very pretty…. Its small round table shone like the mirror over its hearth;…the half-open, crimson-silk door…. The lattice of this room was open; the outer air breathing through, gave freshness, the sweet violets lent fragrance. (*V* 485)

As Zuzanna Jakubowski points out, "the description begins at the 'opening' of an inner door, reveals a 'half-open' door" (98), and the lattice was "open" and "outer" air breathing. The house that M. Paul prepares for Lucy is a space with good ventilation, openness, and no boundaries between inside and outside. According to Piehler, "it is a description of absolute openness, yet one meant to represent the first domestic space Lucy can truly claim as her own" (69). Indeed, it is not in the parlour but "in the balcony outside the French window" that Lucy entertains her benefactor guest, M. Paul, for the first time "as hostess" (*V* 488). Lucy writes: "[t]his balcony was in the rear of the house, the gardens of the faubourg were round us, fields extended beyond" (*V* 488). This balcony is in the 'rear' of the house, similar to her favourite path which is in the 'rear' of the school wall.

Furthermore, the word 'extended beyond' connotes that Lucy will 'extend' her space and behave 'beyond' the societal norm. This openness reveals that Lucy's new house and school will be free from the confinement or regulation that was forced on women during the Victorian age. In addition, as Lucy's house and school are in the city, "the middle of a clean Faubourg" (*V* 484), she can be an onlooker to the citizens in the modernised world. Unlike "the village-school" and the small "cottage" (*JE* 422) that was assigned to Jane Eyre by St John, which was half a mile away from the village, Lucy's house and school make her feel neither desolate nor degraded as Jane's does.

Lucy's last walk with M. Paul is compared to that of Adam and Eve in the Garden of Eden:

> We walked back to the Rue Fossette by moonlight—such moonlight as fell on Eden—shining through the shades of the Great Garden, and haply gilding a path glorious for a step divine—a Presence nameless. Once in their lives some men and women go back to the these first fresh days of our great Sir and Mother—taste that grand

morning's dew—bathe in its sunrise. (*V* 491)

Although Lucy's comparison of their walk to the one in the Great Garden seems to be abrupt, Lucy believes that her future prepared for her by M. Paul is shone by the 'divine' moonlight. According to Lucy Morrison, "the heavy-handed Edenic imagery and other religious resonance in the text are, of course, significant to other thematic veins of the text, but it's the path here that appeals to Lucy and colors her forward motion" (193). Indeed, when Lucy begins her walk with M. Paul, she "scarce knew... whither we rambled" (*V* 484); however, she is certain that their return to Rue Fossette is the path to her independence. Thus, her elation and extreme happiness brought about by acquiring her own space and accepting M. Paul's proposal might be enhanced by the expression of divine resonance.

2.2.2. Travel by Coach and by Sea

Lucy describes her travel to London from the middle of England as follows:

> In going to London, I ran less risk and evinced less enterprise than the reader may think. In fact, the distance was only fifty miles. My means would suffice both to take me there, to keep me a few days, and also to bring me back. (*V* 45)

Excusing herself for going to London by herself, she does not want the readers to make a deal of it and care about the distance to London and her finances. She has already informed us that she has fifteen pounds. A journey of fifty miles by coach and the stay there for a few days are like a pastime. According to Charlotte Mathieson, from the late eighteenth century, "the combined effects of improved technology in road construction, developments in carriage design, and an increase in available revenue from turnpike trusts, gradually reduced the time, danger and discomfort of travelling by road" (3). While Lucy considers her first journey to London to be safe and not costly, it takes her a whole day to reach London. According to Anne D. Wallace, "the fastest coaches of the 1820s and 1830s, the peak era of coach travel in England, averaged about ten miles an hour" (21). Thus, the journey must have taken more time than she expected, for she is dropped off the stagecoach at about nine o'clock on a rainy February night in "a Babylon and a wilderness", confused with "the vastness and the strangeness" (*V* 45) of London. It is remarkable that Lucy does not complain about her long journey on the stagecoach and instead focuses on expressing her bewilderment in finding herself in an unfamiliar space in the metropolitan city by using the metaphor of Babylon, the ancient city in Mesopotamia, to highlight the strangeness and wilderness of London. Even though the people speak English, Lucy complains that she cannot understand "the strange speech" of the cabmen and others waiting around, which seemed to her as "odd as a foreign tongue" (*V* 45). On arriving at the metropolitan city, Lucy undergoes a culture shock upon encountering the cultural differences between the country and the metropolitan city, and she feels that she does not belong in London.

Lucy, in the hotel, happens to gain information regarding a vessel's departure for the continental port—Boue-Marine. Blaming the coachman for dropping her off in the midst of a throng of watermen on the wharf, Lucy views their struggle for her and her trunk as "an uncomfortable crisis" (*V* 50). While she manages to find a boat with two rowers to row to her ship—The Vivid—her isolation is highlighted when she links the black river akin to "a torrent of ink" (*V* 50) to the image of "the Styx" with "Charon rowing some solitary soul to the Land of Shades" (51) from Greek mythology. Her worries and anxieties are intensified by "a chilly wind blowing in my face" and "midnight clouds dropping rain above my head" (*V* 51). While her uncomfortableness continues until an exorbitant fare is demanded by the rude rower on arriving at "the Vivid", she is "animated" by her inner courage rather than being "depressed" (*V* 51). As Brontë later introduces the foreigners' ironical opinion that "it is only English girls who can thus be trusted to travel alone" (*V* 53), she seems to esteem not only the English's generosity in admitting women's travelling alone but also Englishwomen's mobilities to act by themselves with courage despite hardships.

In contrast to the gloomy boat in the River Thames, which was black like ink, the large steam vessel she boards to cross the Straits of Dover named "Vivid" provides Lucy with a clear destination. From the beginning to the latter half of the voyage, while Ginevra Fanshawe and the other passengers feel seasick, Lucy enjoys "liberty" with "the sea-breeze", divining "the delight" from "the heaving Channel waves" (*V* 56) on deck. Ginevra, a talkative and fluffy school-girl in Villette, has studied at several schools in Germany and France as her uncle in France, M. de Bassompierre, pays her school expenses. While Ginevra has crossed the Channel ten times, she complains of seasickness as soon as she gets in sight of the sea. While the other passengers suffer from seasickness throughout the voyage, Lucy does not become sick until the ship approaches the continent. The seasickness from sailing through rough waves is often suggested as a topic related to the risk of modernity. About Brontë's depiction of Lucy's seasickness, Charlotte Mathieson argues that Lucy's seasickness is induced by "a correlation between the proximity of the continent/ distance from England and the growing ill health of the travelers" (99–100). Mathieson continues, "the distance from England and the proximity of the continent" affects "increasing levels of physical discomfort" (100). However, Lucy becomes sick and falters down into the cabin immediately after she imagines that "I saw the continent of Europe, like a wide dream-land, far away", (*V* 56) and the rainbow in the background of the long coast, and then Lucy asks the readers to forget her illusion. I believe that Lucy has already recognised her displacement in England and has no regrets about having left her homeland; therefore, she does not care about the distance from England. Lucy's reference to "day-dreams are delusions of the demon" (*V* 57) after her reverie on the "dream-land" represents her self-mockery of her expectations regarding the continent and serves as a warning to herself. Consequently, I think that her sickness is induced by her self-mockery of her shallow anticipations regarding the new world and serves as a physical warning to herself rather than representing her anxiety about "the proximity of the continent/ distance from England" (Mathieson 99). Moreover, "in another quarter of an hour", the ship comes closer to the port, when "a calm fell upon us all" (*V* 57); that is, all the passengers became free of their seasickness. However, when the vessel arrives at the port, Lucy goes on deck, recognising that she is not welcomed by the continent:

> When I went on deck, the cold air and black scowl of the night seemed to rebuke me for my presumption in being where I was: the lights of the foreign sea-port town, glimmering round the foreign harbour, met me like unnumbered threatening eyes. (*V* 57)

On entering the foreign country, Lucy is greeted by "the cold air" and a "black scowl", which seems to blame her for coming there. Similarly, the glimmering lights around the harbour seem to put her under surveillance with "threatening eyes" (*V* 57). In contrast to the cold welcome received by Lucy, Ginevra and the other passengers are welcomed by their friends and families. The depiction of the foreign country's hostile rejection of Lucy upon her entry makes her recognise that she has no place in the continent. To escape from "the wide and weltering deep" (*V* 60), Lucy, who is desperately grasping at straws, depends on the information provided by Ginevra. Her information that Madame Beck, the principal of her school, seeks an English governess for her children leads Lucy to "her residence" (*V* 60) in Villette, the great capital of the great kingdom of Labassecour.

Her diligence (stagecoach) travels 40 miles from the hotel near the harbour to Villette, slowly through the cold rain. Lucy does not show any interest in the landscape of Labassecour seen through the window of the coach, as the journey is tedious. The scenery, such as the "slimy canals" (*V* 60) beside the road, "formal pollard willows", and "fields" like "kitchen-garden beds" (61) that are artificially preserved and tidily managed by the people, does not attract her. In contrast to the scenery of the middle of England, which Lucy characterised as desert and wilderness, she sees the metropolitan city in the continent as artificial and modern. Closed in the stagecoach, Lucy indulges herself in her reverie through the journey. Brontë seems to daringly offer Lucy a disconnection between her body and the space traversed. It is strange that the foreign landscape, which she experiences for the first time, does not attract her attention. Approaching the suburbs of Villette in darkness amidst thick fog and dense rain, she realises that the stagecoach goes through the gate where soldiers are stationed, stopping at the bureau. Thus, she gets to the safety of the town, which is protected or watched by the soldiers. According to Mathieson, "the networked nation" is created "through the stagecoach" (25). Although her journey by stagecoach was safe enough for her to be absorbed in fancy, Lucy has trouble deboarding the stagecoach. She cannot find her trunk, which must have been stowed in the stagecoach, and cannot ask for help from the coachman as she does not speak French. Indeed, as soon as she exits the stagecoach, she loses the security offered by the networked nation and becomes aware that she might lose her trunk, which contained all her possessions of fifteen pounds. Brontë depicts a similar accident in *Jane Eyre* as well. Jane, escaping from Thornfield by stagecoach, leaves her purse with all her possessions behind in the coach and has to roam in the fields and village without money. However, Lucy happens to have the support of an English gentleman, who negotiates with the coachman in French, and arranges for her to receive it at the bureau after two days. She is informed that her trunk was removed by the coachman and left behind at Boue-Marine along with the other parcels and that it would be forwarded the next day. Therefore, Lucy is not cast out from the communal networked nation in Villette but remains within the modern network of mobility. Thus, the stagecoach functions as a means of connection between one place and another place in the modern networked nation and for the progress of the narratives, though Lucy does not try to create the space between her body and the place she has traversed by stagecoach.

During her stay in La Terrasse, the manor of Dr John Graham Bretton and his mother, Lucy accompanies them to the concert by carriage. While she is worried that the pink dress prepared for her by Mrs Bretton is not suitable for her, she has "a fresh gala feeling" (*V* 208) about her first experience visiting the places of public amusement by carriage. She "liked the drive there well" and had "the snug comfort of the close carriage on a cold though fine night, the pleasure of setting out with companions so cheerful and friendly" (*V* 208). Thus, Lucy places herself in the comfortable carriage and communicates with the space traversed. The landscape Lucy views through the window of the carriage is different from that she had seen or felt while wandering aimlessly about the city in solitude during the summer vacation. "The stars glinting fitfully through the trees as we rolled along the avenue", "the freer burst of the night-sky when we issued forth to the open chaussee", and "the passage through the city gates" (*V* 208) where the soldiers conducted their inspections are all observed, perceived, and relished by Lucy, both physically and mentally. Lucy recognises the places her carriage passes along the city and shares the pleasure with Dr John and Mrs Bretton, who are as kind to her as if she were their relative. However, listening to their animated conversation, Lucy's concern shifts from the landscape of the city to that of Madame Beck's school:

> Our way lay through some of the best streets of Villette, streets brightly lit, and far more lively now than at high noon. How brilliant seemed the shops! How glad, gay, and abundant flowed the tide of life along the broad pavement! While I looked, the thought of the Rue Fossette came across me—of the walled-in garden and school-house, and of the dark, vast "classes", where, as at this very hour, it was my wont to wander all solitary, gazing at the stars through the high, blindless windows, and listening to the voice of the reader. (*V* 208)

Two exclamations represent Lucy's new awareness in Villette. First, it surprises her that the streets in the modernised city are lit by oil street lamps and full of more brilliant shops and more lively people in the evening than at noon. Second, she conjures up a dark image of the confined garden and school building of the Rue Fossette, in contrast to the vivid openness of the city. Riding in the carriage gives Lucy a sense of superiority over the people in the Rue Fossette. According to Mathieson, "owning a carriage or being able to afford coach travel is referenced as a marker of social position" (22). The "shadow of the future" of her listening and wandering "stole with timely sobriety across the radiant present" (*V* 208). Remembering her isolation, which she experienced and will continue to experience, Lucy considers her ride in the carriage with the Brettons a temporary and brief respite for her. As Gilbert and Gubar point out, throughout this chapter, "the bourgeois arts at the concert" are "commercial" (421). That is, Lucy experiences the middle-class art produced in capitalist modernity in the concert. The lustrous and gorgeous atmosphere of the concert hall dazzles Lucy and leaves her unsure about her location and destination. Although Lucy faces a great mirror in the hall, she is unaware of it. Looking at the reflections of Mrs Bretton, Dr John, and herself, Lucy does not recognise them and believes them all to be strangers for an instant.

Consequently, she says, "thus receiving an impartial impression of their appearance. But the impression was hardly felt and not fixed, before the consciousness that I faced a great mirror…dispelled it" (*V* 209). According to Diane Long Hoeveler, although "this sense of seeing oneself as another" (223) is, using Sigmund Freud's expression, "uncanny", "compulsion to repeat is evidenced by Lucy's continual attempts to reinterpret the same characters as if they were different when in fact they are always the same" (224). Looking at the reflection of a woman in a pink dress, Lucy wonders who she is, but she admits that the image in the mirror is also her real self. According to Michel Foucault, the mirror can be both a utopia and a heterotopia:

> [Because] the mirror functions as a heterotopia...it makes this place that I occupy at the moment when I look at myself in the glass at once absolutely real, connected with all the space that surrounds it, and absolutely unreal, since in order to be perceived it has to pass through this virtual point which is over there. (1991; 4)

Lucy seems to understand this dual nature of the mirror, and she realises that the "Lucy" reflected in the mirror is another one, who is far from her real self, but at the same time, her real self. As Gilbert and Gubar argue, "the very opulence of the concert hall testifies to the smugness of the arts and the materialism of the people present" (421). Lucy inwardly criticises the materialism represented by "matrons in velvets and satins, in plums and gems" (*V* 214) and the prudish manners and hypocritical behaviours in the hall. Getting into the carriage after the concert, Lucy feels that it is "as warm and as snug as at a fire-side" (*V* 225–26), even in the very cold and dark night, and feels that she is protected in the carriage. Absorbed in conversation and laughter in the carriage, both the Brettons and Lucy do not notice that the coachman has taken the wrong way until they ride for an hour and a half. When Dr John Bretton realises the situation, he mounts the box of the carriage and takes the reins from the intoxicated coachman. Their safe arrival home is brought about by Dr John's chivalrous behaviour to protect the women. Thus, his action of taking over the reins of the carriage, which has lost its way, symbolises that he navigates Lucy temporally. At the concert, gaining insight regarding the nature of Ginevra Fanshawe, who showed a rude attitude to Mrs Bretton, Dr John conceives her as "neither a pure angel, nor a pure-minded woman" (*V* 218). Released from the illusion of her, he regains his evaluation of Lucy, who has been irritated by Ginevra's trifling with Dr John. In this scene, the coach functions as a means of elevating Lucy's feelings for Dr John.

Lucy's last experience of the coach with Dr John is conceived to be an adventure at first by Lucy but later turns out to be an illusion. In the theatre of Vashti, as soon as the play is over, Lucy and Dr John are involved in the cruel chaos caused by the shouts of fire. Dr John helps a girl who is injured in the stampede. While the beautiful girl is carried into the carriage of M. de Bassompierre, her father, Dr John is asked by him to follow him to provide further medical care. Dr John explains to M. de Bassompierre that Lucy is "neither hindrance nor incumbrance" (*V* 261), and his carriage drives fast to the residence of M. de Bassompierre, the Hotel Crecy. While Lucy and Dr John are silent because of the tense atmosphere during the drive, she feels that she shares "an adventure" (*V* 262) with him. M. de Bassompierre's residence is not an inn, but a vast, lofty apartment, which was once the abode of the prince of Russia. Later, the injured girl turns out to be the seventeen-year-old Polly (Paulina Mary Home). As Lucy notices the girl staring at him, she recognises Dr John as John Graham Bretton, whom the child Polly had loved at the Brettons' house in England. On their way back, Dr John and Lucy pass the theatre again and see that the fire is quenched; however, she realises that the adventure she thought she would experience with Dr John is over. Lucy reacknowledges that she is only an insignificance for Dr John, even if she is not a hindrance.

His carriage carried them back to their past relationship, depriving her of her feelings for him.

2.3. *North and South*
2.3.1. Walking

North and South demonstrates that Margaret Hale is a pedestrian through her assertion when asked by Henry Lennox, at the house on Harley Street, how she spends her time in her hometown, Helstone: "[W]alk, decidedly. We have no horse, nor for papa. He walks to the very extremity of his parish. The walks are so beautiful, it would be a shame to drive—almost a shame to ride" (*NS* 14). According to Charlotte Mathieson, walking experienced "a positive cultural shift" throughout the early nineteenth century; "walking became a popular leisure practice among the upper classes, encapsulating the Romantic ideals of freedom, independence, and communication with nature, and providing space for philosophical reflection and creative thought" (20). Margaret enjoys walking, which connotes that she has an inclination for freedom, nature, and independence. She nurses a grievance against her aunt Shaw for using a carriage: "how tired I used to be of the drives every day in Aunt Shaw's carriage, and how I longed to walk!" (*NS* 20). However, walking is also often linked to poverty, evinced by the fact that Mr Hale not owning a horse is used to reveal his modest livelihood. On returning to her home—Helstone—from Harley Street, Margaret enjoys walking alongside her father through the New Forest, appreciating the fascinating forest, the fragrance of the fern crushed by her foot, and the herbs and flowers. She is proud of the forest and mingles with the inhabitants of the village:

> She [Margaret] made hearty friends with them; learned and delighted in using their peculiar words; took up her freedom amongst them; nursed their babies; talked or read with slow distinctness to their old people; carried dainty messes to their sick; resolved before long to teach at the school where her father went regularly every day as to an appointed task, but she was continually tempted off to go and see the some individual friend—man, woman, or child—in some cottage in the green shade of the forest. (*NS* 19)

Margaret's walking is associated with her philanthropic activity, but her philanthropic activities are undertaken individually; she does not belong to any philanthropic group. She helps people so willingly and voluntarily that her actions go beyond her duties as the daughter of a clergyman. Eleanor Gordon and Gwyneth Nair claim that "religious and philanthropic activity was central to the creation of middle-class identity, as was demonstrating one's good character through good works" (115). However, Margaret does not aid the weak in the recognition of her middle-class identity. Instead, she uses the peculiar dialect of the villagers and desires to assimilate into the community of the forest people because it gives her pleasure. As Lesa Scholl suggests, "language is tied to identity, and by speaking like the other inhabitants, Margaret adapts and begins to belong" (101). Indeed, walking about the forest and talking like the inhabitants allow Margaret to assimilate into the group of the villagers who do not belong to the middle class in Helstone. However, Mrs Hale does not seem to admit the relationship between the villagers and themselves: "I can't help regretting constantly that papa has really no one to associate with here;... seeing no one but farmers and labourers...to week's end" (*NS* 20). Thus, Mrs Hale regrets that they are not involved in middle-class society, but neither Margaret nor Mr Hale cares about class boundaries. In Harley Street, Margaret's human relationship is confined to the private sphere of the middle class, and her bias against "shoppy people" (*NS* 20) or tradespeople must have been bred during her stay in London. According to Dorice Williams Elliott, in the nineteenth century, what is usually called the public sphere was "actually an aggregate of diverse activities and interests encompassing government, education, business, manufacturing, science, and the arts" (26). Therefore, Margaret's teaching activity at the school, which her father regularly visited, belongs to the public sphere, despite her activities at the school being supervised by her father.

Moreover, Elliot argues that when a middle-class woman left her own home to visit the homes of the poor, she used her domestic "'expertise' to authorize herself as an expert, masculinized observer of the social" (27). Thus, Elliot claims that such middle-class women should be "defined as social or, in other words, as at least partly public" (27). I concur with this argument and argue that Margaret's aid of the villagers is performed in the public sphere. Margaret's walking "in spite of the weather" (*NS* 20) is also ascribed to her being tired of hearing her mother's complaint about her beloved father's small income. Mathieson points out that walking provides a woman "a space of privacy away from the confines of home" (30). Even though she feels the confinement in the parsonage, Margaret is "so happy out of doors, at her father's side, that she almost danced" (*NS* 20) and "with the soft violence of the west wind behind her, as she crossed some heath, she seemed to be borne onwards, as lightly and easily as fallen leaf that was wafted along by the autumnal breeze" (21). Margaret thus goes forward, flexibly like a wafted leaf. According to Scholl, while the image presented by this scene is "predominantly pastoral, the violence of the wind reflects the changing world, and the comparison of Margaret to an easily moved leaf acts as a reminder that she is designed for mobility, even though she seeks to ignore that impulse" (99). This demonstrates that Margaret is a mobile woman who loves to walk and goes forward courageously, vigorously, and flexibly even when the world ahead of her is changeable and strict.

Margaret's walks in the parsonage garden present events in which she experiences ordeals. Walking with Lennox in the garden, Margaret is confused with his proposal. As she thought that he understood her the most in London, she is disappointed at his misunderstanding of her nature. Furthermore, the fact that her rejection is unexpected for him hurts her dignity as a lady. However, she regrets that her refusal may impair his pride and her friendship with him. Forced by Mr Hale to take responsibility for informing the invalid mother of the sad news of their move, Margaret walks with her in the garden. Margaret does this because she supposes that Mrs Hale will be shocked and may want to cry without worrying about Dixon or a servant observing her grief. Enduring her agony of their moving, Margaret consoles her mother. Thus, Margaret represents consideration for others even when she has a hard time. On the day before their leaving Helstone, Margaret's walk in the garden differs from what it used to be. Exhausted and distressed by her duty to prepare for their move, she is frightened even by the slightest sound, such as a falling branch. Hearing the poachers' leaping over the garden fences, she becomes afraid for the first time. She used to be excited by "the wild adventurous freedom of their life," even wish for their "success" (*NS* 55). Notably, Margaret wishes for the poachers' success despite their actions against law. Such a transgressive feeling as a middle-class lady connotes her daring behaviour of lying to an inspector to protect her brother in the later of the novel. However, in her walk the evening before leaving Helstone, her original nature of seeking adventure disappears as her sensibility has been weakened physically and mentally. This may stem from her fear of losing her identity as the daughter of Helstone parsonage, having to live in a completely unfamiliar town, and acknowledging the fragility of what she has depended on.

Margaret's frequent walks in Northern Milton are undertaken to help her household in some way, such as securing a house maid to assist Dixon—Mrs Hale's maid—instead of her invalid mother. At first, Margaret is not accustomed to walking by herself in the industrial town with the unfamiliar factory workers:

> Until Margaret had learnt the times of their ingress and egress, she was very unfortunate in constantly falling in with them. They came rushing along with bald, fearless faces, and loud laughs and jests, particularly aimed at all those who appeared to be above them in rank or station. The tones of their unrestrained voices, and their carelessness of all common rules of street politeness, frightened Margaret a little first. (*NS* 72)

In contrast to her leisurely and pleasurable walks in the countryside at Helstone, walking in the busy and bustling streets of Milton is a difficult experience for her. In London, Margaret used to rebel against her aunt, Mrs Shaw's rule that "a footman should accompany Edith and Margaret, if they went beyond Harley Street or the immediate neighbourhood" (*NS* 71). Similarly, in Helstone, Margaret would often enjoy "the free walks and rambles of her forest life" (*NS* 71). In contrast, at Milton, she is annoyed with the workers' outspokenness in the street. However, the humorous remark of one of the lingerers, the middle-aged worker, Higgins, gives Margaret relief: "your bonny face, my lass, makes the day look brighter" (*NS* 72). According to Gaskell's description, Margaret's mouth is wide, but "the wide mouth was one soft curve of rich red lips", and her face "was bright as the morning,—full of dimples, and glances that spoke of childish gladness, and boundless hope in the future" (*NS* 18). Her bright and hopeful face makes a favourable impression on Higgins.

Margaret's casual meeting with Higgins and his daughter, Bessy, in the street, where Margaret gives Bessy flowers that she had just picked, transforms Margaret's negative image of the Northern industrial town Milton into a positive one. Margaret was prejudiced against Northern Milton and the inhabitants in Milton, observing that the people in Milton were dressed with slovenliness and looseness, which are "different from the shabby, threadbare smartness of a similar class in London" (*NS* 60). Recognising that Margaret is from the South, Higgins, who is from Burnley-ways, farther north of Milton, refers to their meeting as follows: "*North and South* has both met and made kind o'friends in this big smoky place" (*NS* 73). This reference has a symbolic meaning within the narrative as Margaret performs the role of a mediator between *North and South*. As for Margaret's encounter with the Higgins family, Gaskell describes that "Milton became a brighter place to her"; "[i]t was not the long, bleak, sunny days of spring, nor yet was it that time was reconciling her to the town of her habitation. It was that in it she had found a human interest" (*NS* 75). According to Abigail Dennis, Margaret, recognising the humanity of its inhabitants, no longer finds Milton threatening; instead, she finds it to be a "habitable space" (48).

Indeed, what Margaret craves is a human relationship in this unfamiliar northern industrial town. Soon after his observation gladdens her, she almost loses his friendship when she offers to visit them. Higgins does not want to invite a female visitor with a philanthropic spirit as he does not believe in God and dislikes religion. Margaret, who is no longer the daughter of the parson in Helstone, recognises the difference of the regions and that her visits to the homes of the poor people are not welcome in the Northern industrial town. As Dorice Williams Elliot argues, "Margaret modifies her attitudes and adapts her charitable practices to fit the new social circumstances she encounters in the industrial North" (32). Thus, Margaret visits the Higgins family not as a philanthropic visitor but as their private friend. Lesa Scholl claims that, from this moment, Margaret can act as "a mediatory force between the two cultures" (100). Margaret gets accustomed to walking along the Northern industrial streets, intermingles with the working-class people, and enters the public social sphere by learning the customs of Northern society.

Margaret's interest in the Higginses and her friendship with Bessy, who, like Margaret, is nineteen years old, leads Margaret to walk frequently to their house. Furthermore, her method of interaction with the working-class people changes from her dealings with the villagers in Helston into more personal and social interactions with the Higginses. Elliott argues that "*North and South* does represent an exemplary woman visitor, and it makes some important claims about her fitness for the role of mediator between classes" (25). Margaret's conversation with the Higgins', where she listens to their complaints about the masters in the factory and the suffering incurred by Bessy from consumption, deepens their relationship and broadens Margaret's perspective on the issues faced by the working class in the factories and industrial towns during the Victorian age. Acquiring intimate knowledge of the wants and habits of the working-class people, which she was unaware of during her stay in the country, arouses Margaret's philanthropic spirit; however, she is distressed at her own helplessness. Margaret's sympathy for Bessy's illness caused by her work in the spinning mill encourages Bessy to think about God; however, this infuriates Higgins. According to Carolyn Lambert, Bessy functions as a double for Margaret: "her journey towards death mirrors Margaret's journey towards maturity, and it is the link with Bessy and her family that acts as the catalyst for changing Margaret's perceptions, values, and assessment of the world around her" (56). Bessy loves to hear Margaret speak about the greenery-filled landscape of her home—Helstone, believes in God despite Higgins' displeasure, and expects that she will go to Heaven after her death, like Helen in *Jane Eyre*. Margaret is also consoled by talking to Bessy about her beloved home, which satisfies her nostalgia for Helstone. Margaret's actions of helping the feverish Bessy to drink a cup of water, lifting her hair from off her temples, and bathing them with water, reveal not only her affection towards Bessy but also her ingrained caring attitude akin to that of a nurse, which was gained through domestic expertise and philanthropic experience; her devoted actions move both Bessy and Higgins. Their conversations about the factory, the strike, and the union are so closely related to the hardships of their life that it blurs the boundaries between their private and public lives.

Additionally, the diagnosis of Mrs Hale's serious health condition from the doctor makes Margaret uneasy, and she engages in walking inside the house for a while as a diversion; however, as she cannot alter her distressed state of mind, she decides to take a walk:

[T]he length of a street—yes, the air of Milton Street—cheered young blood before she reached her first turning. Her step grew lighter, her lips redder. She began to take notice, instead of having her thoughts turned so exclusively inward. She saw unusual loiterers in the streets. (*NS* 131)

According to Abigail Dennis, "as she embarks on active exploration of the city streets, Margaret begins to observe as well as to be observed, thus initiating a process of identification with the external urban environment (and, by extension, its inhabitants)" (48). While walking "along the crowded narrow streets" (*NS* 100) toward Bessy's house, Margaret recognises that she turns her interest to the industrial city as well as its occupants. According to Carolyn Lambert, "[Margaret's] journeys around Milton and her visits to the Higgins family may be viewed as a version of the pastoral role her father undertook in Helstone as well as a comment on the role of the domestic visitor" (89). According to Collins dictionary, pastoral role refers to "the pastoral duties of a priest or other religious leader, which involves looking after the people he or she has responsibility for, especially by helping them with their personal problems" ("Pastoral," def. 1). Margaret, in Milton, takes on Mr Hale's role as a clergyman who used to walk to the extremities of Helstone, and visits the Higginses and later the widow and children of Boucher, a strikebreaker. However, her interactions with the inhabitants of working-class households prompt her to examine their working environments, domestic space, and human relationships with their colleagues and masters. In contrast to her cowardly father, Margaret is strong and courageous enough to face the tragedy of Boucher's suicide after the attack at Thornton's mill. Margaret is more deeply involved within the space of the industrial city, which has both social problems arising from modernity and private sufferings, than Mr Hale, an ex-clergyman.

In Milton, Margaret visits not only the working-class neighbourhood of the Higgins family but also the Thorntons in Marlborough Street. Thornton is a manufacturer and a favoured pupil of Mr Hale. The nature of the relationship between the Hales and the Thorntons is of the middle class, which includes visits and dinners. When Margaret and Mr Hale visit the Thorntons for the first time, they are perplexed by the unfamiliar industrial streets. Walking about two miles from Margaret's house in Crampton—a suburb of Milton—to Marlborough Street, they cannot find a house large enough for the habitation of the apparently wealthy Mrs Thornton. While Margaret imagines that the "tall, massive, handsomely dressed Mrs Thornton must live in a house of the same character as herself" (*NS* 111), in Marlborough Street, they can only see small houses and a blank wall. Inquiring to a passer-by for directions to Thornton's house, they are informed that the Thorntons live at the end of the long wall, within the factory lodge door where a lodge-keeper stands, in the big house situated within the same premises as the big factory. Both Margaret and Mr Hale are surprised at the sounds of "the continual clank of machinery", "the long groaning roar of the stream-engine", and on seeing the offices for business and "the immense many-windowed mill", when walking through the great oblong yard that takes them to "the handsome stone-coped house" (*NS* 111) of the Thorntons. This is probably Margaret and Mr Hale's first time seeing the factory up close. Margaret wonders why the Thorntons, who are a wealthy family of manufacturers, do not live in the quiet suburbs. Margaret's wonderment arises from the middle-class ideals of the Victorian age. According to Charlotte Mathieson, "there was an increase in workers living further from workplace—encouraged among the middle classes by the growth of the suburbs" (7). While the reason Mrs Thornton lives at the site of the mill is not described, she is so proud of her son and his work that she does not care about the noise of the factory. Receiving the invitation, Margaret and Mr Hale attend Mrs Thornton's dinner. Although she is reluctant to go due to her mother's illness and Bessy's miserable physical condition, Margaret is persuaded by Mrs Hale to observe how dinner is managed in Milton. At Mrs Thornton's dinner, Margaret notices that the drawing room is arranged differently compared to their first visit: "every cover was taken off" in the room, and "the yellow silk damask and a brilliantly-flowered carpet" and too much ornament become "a weariness to the eye" (*NS* 159). Acquiring a cultivated taste in London, Margaret feels the delicacies offered for dinner oppressive and its quantity too large and regards Mrs Thornton's dinner as being far from elegant. Margaret recognises that such brilliance based on Mrs Thornton's ostentation represents "a strange contrast to the bald ugliness of the look-out into the great mill-yard" (*NS* 159). Although Thornton's house, situated within the factory premises, is always full of noisy sounds from the machines, the strike by the workers has stopped the movement of the machines. She begins to encounter complicated emotions as she realises the reasons for the workers' strike and the extreme poverty that some of them, like Boucher, are subject to on account of not receiving a salary due to the strike. Simultaneously, Margaret thinks "how much she enjoyed this dinner" because "she knew enough now to understand many local interests—nay, even some of the technical words employed by the eager millowners" (*NS* 162). While other guests or ladies are interested in the distinctive elegance of Margaret's white silk attire, Margaret thinks that their interests are trivial and wants to listen to "something larger and grander" and feels "the exultation in the sense of power which these Milton men have" (*NS* 162). Thus, Margaret has a hybrid nature that combines the feminine beauty and decency of a middle-class lady and a masculine interest in power. Moreover, while she has the decency of a middle-class lady, she sympathises with the working-class people as if she were a factory woman. At the dinner, Margaret gets to understand not only the energetic interest of the millowners in their manufacturing activities and trade but also their confrontations with the workers, which was a regular occurrence in the modernised industrial town. She is satisfied with belonging to the social and public sphere of Milton and walks back home with her father excitedly; she is described as tucking up her silk to her knee and being "ready to dance with the excitement of the cool, fresh night air" (*NS* 164).

While she is enjoying her walk through Milton Street, Margaret observes the unusual situations of the unemployed people in the street. Instead of walking in the field around her house, Margaret visits the Higgins family and learns of the strike from Bessy, who describes the misery of the previous strikes. Higgins, a member of the union, complains that against the union's plan, lots of strike breakers, who are angry at not receiving any wages due to the strike and at Thornton's employment of Irish workers, are planning on marching to Marlborough Mill. Margaret perceives that a serious matter, which has not occurred previously in the country, is approaching this industrial city. Thus, Margaret is involved in "a battle between the two classes" (*NS* 84) through her associations with both classes. As Anthony Giddens argues, "modernity...produces differences, exclusion and marginalization" (6), and Margaret sees that the modernised industrial city produces the inequality she has observed. Margaret's personal walks outdoors seeking diversion leads her to the blurred space between the private and public sphere, irrespective of her intentions.

Margaret's errand to borrow a waterbed for her invalid mother from Mrs Thornton coincides with the day the rioters proceed to Thornton's large house and factory on Marlborough Street. Margaret is absorbed by her anxiety that she may lose her mother and, therefore, fails to notice the restless sense of irritation among the people in the street during her two-mile walk from her house. As she approaches Marlborough Street, she sees the enraged workers roaring low and marching, and she quickly goes up the steps of Thornton's house, finding no steam engine working. She is shown into Mrs Thornton's drawing room on the second floor, where she finds the women gathered around the windows, engrossedly observing the scene that terrifies them due to the workers' angry voices and the sounds of the maddened crowd's attempts to destroy the great gates of the mill. Margaret notices that even Mrs Thornton, who urged Margaret to "learn to have a brave heart" (*NS* 116) in Milton, shows her terror and that her fingers tremble when shutting the windows. While Mrs Thornton is proud of her courage, the tremendous roars of the rioters make her retreat to the back room of the drawing room with Fanny, her daughter, who has fainted. Hiding the Irish workers in the factory, Thornton seems "noble" with "a proud look of defiance on his face" (*NS* 173) and urges Margaret to go secure herself upstairs. Waiting in the drawing room for the arrival of soldiers to disperse the rioters, he does not try to go out until Margaret encourages him to talk with the workers outside the house. As Simon Morgan points out, "Mr Thornton's masculinity is questioned" (185). Unlike Thornton and Mrs Thornton, Margaret shows her courage because she knows the rage of the rioters: "she knew how it was; they were like Boucher,...

Margaret knew it all; she read it in Boucher's face, forlornly desperate and livid with rage" (*NS* 176). Margaret has heard Higgins revile the strikebreaking of Boucher—Higgins' neighbour, who cannot feed his many children due to not receiving a salary. As Abigail Dennis argues, "Margaret's experiences on the city streets and in the homes of the poor have given her a perspective advantage" (49). Urging Thornton to speak with his workers outside, Margaret fastens the door after he goes out to protect Mrs Thornton and Fanny and returns to "her place by the farthest window" (*NS* 175). Opening the window to observe him on the steps, Margaret "tore her bonnet off" (*NS* 176) to hear him. According to Morgan, "tearing off the bonnet reveals that Margaret abandons the passive, decorative femininity" (185). Indeed, Margaret tries to aggressively involve herself in the industrial dispute by tearing a bonnet, the symbol of femininity. On seeing some young men preparing to throw their wooden clogs as missiles towards Thornton, Margaret leaves the window, rushes out of the drawing room, and goes out of the house to stand between the angry workers and Thornton at the step of the house. Morgan argues that "Margaret's abandonment of her position at the window, with its connotations of sexual purity, links to a symbolical fallen woman" (186). I disagree with Morgan's argument. Margaret leaves the security of Mrs Thornton's drawing room into the perilous and secular space outside the house due to her sense of responsibility in having persuaded him to enter the dangerous situation and her instinctive courage to protect an outnumbered man. As Patsy Stoneman suggests, Margaret's action of protecting Thornton by throwing her arms around him on seeing a pebble fly towards him is brought about by a "humanitarian motive" (84). Margaret rejects Thornton's proposal later by insisting that she owes her action to women's nature: "any women, worthy of the name of women, would come forward to shield, with her reverenced helplessness, a man in danger from the violence of the numbers" (*NS* 193). Thus, Margaret always sides with the weak as evidenced by her philanthropic activities. According to Stoneman, "Margaret's intervention in the riot is as unacceptable as a caring act as it is an act of sexual provocation; both are inappropriate to a scene defined in terms of warfare" (90). However, as Divya Athmanathan argues, Margaret's intervention in the industrial riot leads to her "involvement in the public sphere" (42). Margaret becomes involved in the public sphere by acting as a negotiator with the rioters: "The soldiers are sent for—are coming. Go peaceably.... You shall have relief from your complaints, whatever they are" (*NS* 177). Margaret's actions not only represent her sympathy for the workers, who had become rioters, but also her desire to help Thornton, who is in danger. Her fainting from being struck by the pebble pelted by a worker and the blood on her forehead causes the rioters to regain their reason and retreat towards the gate before the arrival of the soldiers. Thus, Margaret's intervention in the riot saves the lives of both Thornton and the rioters. According to Morgan, "Gaskell is clearly criticizing the chivalric model of female influence in making Margaret feel guilty about the violence she has unwittingly encouraged" (185). However, even though Margaret is injured and Fanny and the servants misunderstand her action, Margaret's actions allow her to leave the drawing room, a private, secure place, courageously and voluntarily into the public sphere. While she is unsuccessful in mediating the class struggle between the manufacturers and the workers, who face several social problems in the modernising industrial town, her intervention demonstrates to Thornton that the master needs to talk with his workers, and ultimately leads to Thornton's endeavour to build a dining-room for his workers toward the end of the novel. As Dorice Williams Elliott argues, when Margaret marries Thornton, "like the dining-room that domesticates the factory, Margaret's home blurs the boundaries between the public and private spheres" (48). Thus, Margaret's walk and actions blur the boundaries between the private and the public spheres.

Margaret's invitation of Higgins to her house after Bessy's death also blurs the boundary between classes. Margaret initially hesitates to go see the dead Bessy when informed of Bessy's death by her sister, as Margaret has not seen a dead person before. As Davidoff and Hall argue, "by 1840… women were beginning to be considered too delicate to bear the public rituals of death" (408), so it is not strange that Margaret is afraid of seeing the dead. However, her kindness and compassion urge her to immediately walk to see the dead Bessy at Higgins' house. Finding the dead Bessy's face with a soft smile, Margaret feels glad to have come and observes that the dead look more peaceful than the living. Discovering that Higgins was going out to drown his grief in drink, Margaret obstructs him decidedly and suggests that he should pay his respects to the dead and see Mr Hale, a former clergyman, at her house. Mrs Hale's maid, Dixon complains that Margaret has ushered a working-class man into the study. While Mr Hale is dismayed to hear that Higgins is a drunken infidel weaver at first, he treats Higgins as he does "his all fellow-creatures alike", listening to him with interest (*NS* 222). Similarly, Higgins straightens his appearance before seeing Mr Hale, with a "good, earnest composure on his face" (*NS* 222), and speaks about religion, the masters, and the workers' union frankly. Higgins is embittered not only because Bessy died of a lung disease that she contracted from working in the harsh conditions of the mill but also by the severe circumstances endured by workers in the capitalist modernity. Recognising his dreary feeling, Margaret, touching his arm very softly, consoles him: "we do not want to reason—we believe; and so do you. It is the one sole comfort in such times" (*NS* 224). Mr Hale suggests to Higgins that he should join them in family prayer. In Mr Hale's study, "Margaret the Churchwoman, her father the Dissenter, Higgins the Infidel, knelt down together. It did them no harm" (*NS* 230). A recurring theme within the novel is that human beings are equal before God despite the difference in classes, religions, and opinions. Margaret plays the role of a mediator between the middle and working class. Patsy Stoneman argues that "Elizabeth Gaskell does not suggest that verbal communication will eliminate class struggles" (80). However, Margaret's straight-speaking ability and body language appeal to Higgins' rigid thinking and emotion and consoles his unbearable sorrow; he accepts Margaret's cordial kindness, tries not to drink to fulfil Bessy's last wish, and later in the narrative, receives Mr Hale's bible from Margaret. Thus, Gaskell presents the possibilities of verbal communication between different classes, religions, and regions.

While the instances described in previous sections demonstrate Margaret's ability to access the public sphere, she sometimes also appropriates private spaces to help the powerless. When the drowned body of Boucher, who commits suicide in despair, is carried into the middle of the road by some police officers, only Margaret volunteers to inform his wife of the tragic news. While Higgins and Mr Hale hesitate, Margaret courageously knocks at the door of Boucher's cottage, opens the door, "went in, shutting it after her, and even, unseen to the woman (Boucher's wife), fastening the bolt" (*NS* 289). According to Carolyn Lambert, doors are "barriers which can be used to comment on gendered space and restrictions placed on women" (41). Margaret, in this scene, supposes that Mrs Boucher will lose her self-control at the news of her husband's death and wishes to protect the miserable widow and her little children's privacy from the curiosity of the public eye. Margaret offers Mrs Boucher her protection rather than the restrictions of a gendered space. By closing the door and fastening the bolt, Margaret secures the private space to speak alone to Mrs Boucher without being interrupted by the public. I think that Gaskell uses the locking of the doors as a barrier to create a private space for Margaret and Mrs Boucher.

When the inspector visits her to inquire whether she has accompanied a young gentleman (Frederick) who is suspected of having murdered Leonards at the station, she lies in a dignified manner in the study to protect her brother. After the inspector leaves, Margaret goes half-away into the study, "as if moved by some passionate impulse, and locks the door inside" (*NS* 269) and loses consciousness and falls prone on the floor. Margaret's locking of the door of the house reveals her intention to expel the public power of the police from her private and secure domestic space by playing the role of the patriarch. At the same time, Thornton is consoling Mr Hale, who is depressed by his wife's death, in the drawing room, which is a feminised space. Although Lambert argues that Mr Hale's "study still offers her protection" (40), Margaret does not expect her father's help as she takes on a patriarchal role within her family by using his study. Margaret uses the study as a space that is representative of the Hales when she assumes the responsibility for Frederick's secret return to England following the inquest. Thus, Margaret uses the study, which is part of the masculine sphere, to talk with the inspector and then returns there to keep her physical condition private. This utilisation of the study signifies Margaret's hybrid nature that combines both masculinity and femininity.

Gaskell illustrates Margaret's emotional agitation by describing her movement. When Mrs Thornton visits Crampton to warn Margaret that she should not have walked with a young man in the evening at the station, Margaret becomes indignant and leaves her in the room. Confining herself to her room, Margaret "began to walk backwards and forwards, in her old habitual way of showing agitation" (*NS* 314). Here, the description of "her old habitual way of showing agitation" reveals that Margaret would often walk about in the room when she cannot bring her excitement under control. It can be surmised that Margaret meets Mrs Thornton in the drawing room near her own room as she recognises that "in that slightly-built house every step was heard from one to another, she sat down" (*NS* 314) to avoid Mrs Thornton noticing her footsteps. The contrast between her self-possession during her meeting with the inspector in the study, which is a masculine space, and Margaret's agitation upon hearing Mrs Thornton's comments on her feminine decency in the drawing room signifies that she has feminine sensibility.

Margaret's visit to Helstone with Mr Bell, her godfather, after her parents' death leads her to discover the changes to her home. Margaret's cherished nostalgia for Helstone is premised on her belief that her beloved home would never change. Upon taking a walk with him, she notices that the landscape has changed after she had left with her parents three years previously. Finding old trees felled and a familiar cottage pulled down, she misses the landscape from the past. However, Mr Bell, a Fellow at Oxford, regards this change as natural:

> 'It is the first changes among familiar things that makes such a mystery of time to the young, afterwards we lose the sense of mysterious. I take changes in all I see as a matter of course. The

instability of all human things is familiar to me, to you it is new and oppressive.' (*NS* 378–79)

According to Wendy Parkins, "Bell sees in every change only the eternal verities of age and experience"; in fact, "such transformations have taken place even in a place as close to nature as Helstone confirms for him that change is an inevitable, organic—rather than historical—process" (2004; 511). Although Margaret also accepts the change to be an inevitable, organic process, she is disappointed at the improvements made to the village:

> Places were changed—a tree gone here, a bough there, bringing in a long ray of light where no light was before—a road was trimmed and narrowed, and the green straggling pathway by its side enclosed and cultivated. A great improvement it was called; but Margaret sighed over the old picturesqueness, the old gloom, and the grassy wayside of former days. (*NS* 384)

As Parkins points out, "it is not an unmediated nature which Margaret mourns but an ideal cultivated in a slightly earlier period of modernity; it is the passing of "old picturesqueness" in favour of the new discourses of "improvement" which is lamented" (2004; 511). Margaret loves Helstone and describes it as "a village in a poem—in one of Tennyson's poems" (*NS* 14). She is nostalgic about Helstone because it holds cherished memories related to her parents, who are now dead; thus, she does not want to see it change. When Margaret and Mr Bell visit the parsonage where the Hales used to live, she finds that it is "altered, both inside and out" (*NS* 383) and that a new nursery is under construction.

Mrs Hepworth, the new Vicar's wife, and the Vicar, a teetotaller magistrate who makes sure the villagers do not drink, call the renovations undertaken in the parsonage "improvements" (*NS* 383). According to Divya Athmanathan, building a nursery out of Margaret's room is "telling in the context of spatial demarcation" and "spatial segregation within domesticity in the name of discipline and order" (40). According to Anthony Giddens, "modernity...produces difference, exclusion and marginalization. Holding out the possibility of emancipation, modern institutions at the same time create mechanisms of suppression, rather than actualization, of self" (6). While Mrs Hepworth likes regulations, their seven children mess up the garden, with their hat almost breaking the rose tree nurtured by the Hales during their stay. Furthermore, Mr and Mrs Hepworth's education and discipline of their children are dubious. According to Leonore Davidoff and Catherine Hall, "[G]ardens were used as teaching devices. Children were given small plots to inculcate patience, care, tenderness, and reverence along with practical science lessons" (373). Wendy Parkins argues that "the arrival of the new evangelical clergyman itself is a sign of modernity and transition in the established church" (2004; 511). While the reason for Mr Hale leaving the church is ambiguous within the early sections of the novel, it is possible that he might not have been able to come to terms with the new current of the church.

Throughout *North and South*, characters who cannot accept the changes brought about by time, the difference of regions, and modernity, such as Mr Hale, Mrs Hale, and Mr Bell, die or retreat from the narration. Mr Bell does not like Milton, his birthplace, complaining that "I don't believe there's a man in Milton who knows how to sit still, and it is a great art" (*NS* 323). Margaret suggests that "Milton people, I suspect, think Oxford men don't know how to move" (*NS* 323). As Parkins points out, "the associations here between immobility/tradition and mobility/modernity create a dichotomy in which these polarized positions seem irreconcilable" (2004; 512). Unlike these people, Margaret is more accepting changes:

> Looking out of myself, and my own painful sense of change, the progress all around me is right and necessary. I must not think so much of how circumstances affect me myself, but how they affect others, if I wish to have a right judgement, or a hopeful trustful heart. (*NS* 391)

Taking a walk in Helstone, Margaret recognises that the change and improvement around her is necessary to modernise society. She recognises that it is important that she observes carefully whether she and other people act rightly in the changing world. She notices herself changing: "[A]nd I too change perpetually...now disappointed and peevish because all is not exactly as I had pictured it, and now suddenly discovering that the reality is far more beautiful than I had imagined it" (*NS* 391). Thus, Margaret is not only realising that she will change within the flux of the changing world but is also hopeful of the possibilities of the future in modernity; furthermore, she is cognisant of her own position within the changing society.

Margaret's inheritance of Mr Bell's fortune following his sudden death makes her reconsider how she should behave as an independent woman in the changing world. At Mr and Mrs Lennox's and Mrs Shaw's recommendation, Margaret goes with them to Cromer, the English seaside health resort, to recover physically and mentally. As Charlotte

Mathieson argues, in those days, "domestic travel for health also emerged, first evident in the popularity of spa towns and then in the growth of the seaside resort" (3). As she took her invalid mother to Heston before going to the smoky Milton, Margaret herself is so distressed subsequently by the death of several familiar people that she acknowledges her need for physical and mental rest. In contrast to Mrs Shaw's shopping and Edith and Captain Lennox's riding, Margaret sits on the beach silently looking at the sea:

> She used to sit long hours upon the beach, gazing intently on the wave as they chafed with the perpetual motion against the pebbly shore, —or she looked out upon the more distant heave, and sparkle against the sky, and heard, without being conscious of hearing, the eternal psalm, which went up continually. She was soothed without knowing how or why. Listlessly she sat there, on the ground, her hands clasped round her knees. (*NS* 404)

Observing the movements of the waves, which break on the shore and retreat, Margaret thinks about her past, present, and future. The waves chafing against the pebbly shores represent the people who had passed and the fragility of human life. While despondent about the tragedies of their death, Margaret also feels a sense of elevation from hearing the psalms being recited in the distance. Left alone on the beach, without being distracted by Mrs Shaw, and Mr and Mrs Lennox, Margaret can reflect on her past and future; "[B]ut all this time for thought enabled Margaret to put events in their right places, as to origin and significance, both as regarded her past life and her future" (*NS* 404). As Mr Bell argues that to sit still is "a great art" (*NS* 323), sitting on the beach contemplating the sea and meditating makes an effect on Margaret physically and mentally. According to Anthony Giddens, "modernity is a post-traditional order, in which the question, 'How shall I live?' has to be answered in day-to-day decisions about how to behave, what to wear and what to eat—and many other things—as well as interpreted within the temporal unfolding of self-identity" (14). Thus, Margaret, who is an occupant of the modern world, overcomes the sorrow brought by the death of her beloved people and contemplates what she ought to do for the powerless. She begins to learn about Mr Bell's business from Lennox as she is his heiress, and proclaims upon returning from Cromer to London, that "I shall be merrier than I have ever been, now I have got my own way" (*NS* 407). Margaret is now self-confident as an independent woman and responds to Edith's offer in the back drawing room, which is linked to Edith's femininity, by stating, "I mean to buy them (my dresses) for myself. You shall come with me if you like; but no one can please me but myself" (*NS* 407). Thus, conceiving what she wants to do, Margaret decides to participate in the world of modernity and offer a large investment to Thornton's mill, which is now in dire financial circumstances. Margaret brings the public sphere of business affairs into the private drawing room. Her action dismantles the segregation of spaces and, thus, transgresses the norms of the Victorian era. Upon accepting Thornton's proposal, Margaret becomes involved in the management of the factory, business, and dining for the workers. Thus, she finds her position in the modern industrial town and attains vigorous mobility within modernity.

2.3.2. Travel by Rail and Coach

The Hales' travel by train from Helstone to Milton reflects the developing networks of railways in those days. According to Tim Cresswell, the advent of the railway occurred in 1830 with the Liverpool to Manchester line and much of the major current railway networks were established by 1860 (16). Trains transported not only materials and goods, but also passengers, and the railroad was seen as a symbol of technological and scientific progress. According to Henri Lefebvre, "undeniably, the railways played a fundamental role in industrial capitalism and the organization of its national (and international) space" (212). As the Hales approach the industrial city, Milton, by rail, Margaret notices the changing landscape and smell from the train window:

> For several miles before they reached Milton, they saw a deep lead-coloured cloud hanging over the horizon in the direction in which it lay…. Nearer to the town, the air had a faint taste and smell of smoke; perhaps, after all, more a loss of fragrance of grass and herbage than any positive taste or smell. (*NS* 60)

The scenery from the window of the train bound for the northern industrial city is affected by the smoke and smell from the factories enabling industrial capitalism. As Abigail Dennis points out, "Margaret finds herself disoriented and overwhelmed, by its geography" (46). Margaret is also confused by the approach of the train to the industrial town in disregard of her feeling.

John Urry suggests that "the railway system is central to modernity's appearance" and claims that "the new railways had the effect of 'compress' time and space" (96) owing to the speed of the trains with the power of steam. In those days, clocks and watches were widespread among the people, and as many people began to move on business or for leisure, "by around 1847 the railway companies...adopted Greenwich Mean Time" (Urry 97). Thus, the first railway timetable was published in 1838 (Urry 97), however, while convenient for both operators and passengers, the timetable constrains them. Gaskell highlights not only the rapid speed of the train but also the oppressiveness of the timetable during the Hales' journey from the idyllic southern countryside to the northern industrial city:

> Railroad time inexorably wrenched them away from lovely, beloved Helstone, the next morning. They were gone; they had seen the last of the long low parsonage home, half-covered with China-roses and pyracanthus—more homelike than ever in the morning sun that glittered on its windows, each belonging to some well-loved room. Almost before they had settled themselves into the car, sent from Southampton to fetch them to the station, they were gone away to return no more. (*NS* 57)

The train is more punctual than the stagecoach and does not allow people the time to bemoan their departure from a place. Gaskell depicts the railway as a crueller form of transportation than the stagecoach, which provides time for people to be sentimental regarding the beloved landscape surrounding their homes. The railroad, which "inexorably wrenched them away" from an older period, forcibly transports the Hale family to the modernised city occupying a new age. George Beard considers the modern conception of time to be dangerous:

> The perfection of clocks and the invention of watches have something to do with modern nervousness, since they compel us to be on time,

and excite the habit of looking to see the extra moment, so as not to be late for trains or appointments. Before the general use of these instruments of precision in time, there was a wider margin for all appointments, a longer period was required and prepared for, especially in travelling—coaches of the olden period were not expected to start like steamers or trains, on the instant. (61)

This anxiety, caused by the punctuality of the train, makes modern people nervous. Gaskell acknowledges that the trains' punctuality strains the nerves of the people in the Victorian age. According to Mathieson, "the railway time-table produced a new sense of 'railway time' as regulated and systematised" (8). Later in the narrative, Gaskell creates a similar setting related to the train's punctuality. In visiting Helstone with Mr Bell, her godfather, Margaret becomes afraid that she shall be late for the train: "her last alarm was lest they should be too late and miss the trains; but no! they were all in time" (*NS* 375). While her preparation for the journey is completed long before the appointed time, she is nervous that they might miss the train. Her uneasiness appears to arise from her excitement regarding seeing her beloved home, her anxiety about returning there as an orphan, and her apprehension of being brought back to an older age by the train. At this moment, Mr Bell takes out insurance for Margaret during their travel: "I'll give you back safe and sound, barring railway accidents, and I'll insure your life for a thousand pounds before starting" (*NS* 374). Mr Bell, the tutor at the college of Oxford, thinks that a railway accident could happen and recognises the danger of a train journey. Thus, Gaskell often uses the train, which is a signifier of modernity, as a device to portray the characters' nervousness and uneasiness.

As for the railway accident, Margaret is indirectly involved in the incident between Frederick, her brother, and Leonards. When she sees Frederick off, who the Navy wants for being a ringleader of the riot, he is nearly caught at the station by Leonards, the sailor. Frederick's attempts to avoid him lead to Leonards' fall from the platform and his mysterious death. Although Frederick does not let him fall on purpose, he is suspected of murder by the inspector after he leaves Milton. It is evident from this episode that Margaret fears that Leonards might catch Frederick and that Leonards might have gotten hit by the train. Thus, in *North and South*, the railway network is associated with danger and death. In Cranford, Gaskell also depicted the episode in which Captain Brown is killed in a train accident. As Cresswell points out, "just as the railway was instrumental in ordering modern life through the production of abstract time and abstract space, so it was the source of new anxieties" (20). However, Margaret depends on the train to go home after the unfortunate events at the station. Even after seeing Frederick off, Margaret is so afraid lest Leonards should discover her that she "felt she could not walk home along the road" and decides to get in "the down train" and takes "her seat in it" (*NS* 259) to calm herself. Thus, despite initially associating the railroad with the image of uneasy transportation, Margaret comes to regard the train as a solace for her body weakened by terror and accepts the security of the modernised railroad when she is civilly helped into a carriage by a porter. Consequently, Margaret is engulfed in modernity through the train.

In contrast to the new anxieties created by the railways, the development of railway and other transport networks urged the people "from the upper classes to the middle classes and beyond" to spend "the seaside holiday" (2004; 514), as Wendy Parkins argues. Margaret's plan to take her invalid mother to the bathing-place town of Heston to "get a breath of sea air to set her up for the winter" (*NS* 52) is an effect of the medical beliefs of the period. As Parkins suggests, "the belief in the healthful benefits of visiting the seaside was itself a modern phenomenon" (2004; 514). The Hales reach Heston via a little branch railway from Milton and find Heston to be different from the small bathing places in the south of England. Margaret recognises something "purposelike" (*NS* 59), which stems from the prevailing attitude in the industrial town:

> The country cars had more iron, and less wood and leather about the horse-gear; the people in the streets, although on pleasure bent, had yet a busy mind. The colours looked grayer—more enduring, not so gay and pretty. (*NS* 59)

Even the seaside resorts "bear the marks of the industrial capitalism, which defines Darkshire" (2004; 514), as Parkins points out. Indeed, Margaret, who is from the south, observes that the cars and people in the northern seashore are affected by the modernisation of the nearby industrialised town—Milton. Thus, Margaret recognises that the northern seashore differs from the southern ones before reaching their modernised destination. Marshall Berman explains modernity by adapting Karl Marx's arguments:

> To be modern is to find ourselves in an environment that promises us adventure, power, joy, growth, transformation, of ourselves and the world—and, at the same time, that threatens to destroy everything we have, everything we know, everything we are. Modern environ-

ments and experiences cut across all boundaries of geography and ethnicity, of class and nationality, of religion and ideology: in this sense, modernity can be said to unite all mankind. But it is a paradoxical unity, a unity of disunity: it pours us all into a maelstrom of perpetual disintegration and renewal, of struggle and contradiction, of ambiguity and anguish. To be modern is to be part of a universe in which, as Marx said, "all that is solid melts into air". (15)

As Berman explains the experience of modernity, Margaret cuts across the boundaries of geography, of region between north and south by railway, the modernised transportation; however, she is poured into "a maelstrom of perpetual disintegration and renewal, of struggle and contradiction, of ambiguity and anguish" (Berman 15). Recognising the difference between the northern people and things and those of the south, she is not only confused, but also develops an aversion to the value of the former cultivated by industrialisation. Using Marx's reference that modernity is to be part of a universe where "all that is solid melts in air", Berman's modernity is not static but mobile and fluid. Throughout the narrative of Margaret's mobility from south to north, her inner and outer spaces are disintegrated and experience struggle, ambiguity, and renewal in a society that moves towards modernity. As Tim Creswell argues that "it (Berman's modernity) is not an enemy of mobility but its friend" (18), Margaret's visit to Heston, the southern seashore, offers the opportunity to acknowledge how the people are included by modernity.

When Mr Hale and Margaret drive by coach through the largest street in Milton, when they go house-hunting, Margaret notices the difference between the scenery of the industrial town and that of London. In Milton, there are a lot of factories with chimneys that emit black smoke, and the main street is jammed by vans, wagons, and trucks bearing cotton and calico, which are to be loaded on to the train. Looking out from the coach's window, Margaret feels that even the people thronging the footpath are dressed in more of "a slovenly looseness" (*NS* 60) than those in London. Experiencing displacement upon leaving her home in the South unwillingly, Margaret has embraced the sense of disintegration, contradiction, and ambiguous anguish within herself; however, her drive in Milton serves as her entry into the modern space.

Her prejudice against commerce and manufacture can be gleaned from her observation that "I don't like shoppy people.... I like all people whose occupations have to do with land; I like soldiers and sailors, and the three learned professions, as they call them" (*NS* 20). Even when Mrs Hale states that the Gormans, their neighbour, are very respectable coach-builders, Margaret counters that coach-building is only a trade. She is reprimanded by Mr Hale for calling the Milton manufacturers tradespeople. Margaret's "quiet coldness of demeanour", which is represented through the scene of her first meeting with Thornton, evidences her "contemptuousness" for him (*NS* 64). The house-hunt by coach reveals to Margaret that thirty pounds a year is not enough money for them to rent satisfactory accommodation with two sitting rooms and four bedrooms in Milton. Margaret recommends the house with three sitting rooms in Crampton as a compromise plan to her father. According to Charlotte Mathieson, "Britain was becoming a more mobile population, with migration from rural to urban areas steadily growing from the late eighteenth century" (3); this led to a shortage in the availability of homes to rent in the industrial town, and thereby causes the Hales' difficulty in acquiring their ideal house that satisfies their demands regarding both rent and number of rooms. However, Margaret's elaborate allocation of the rooms by donning the role of the mistress of the house makes it possible to allocate the rooms satisfactorily. Her contrivance is to allocate the front room downstairs for both the dining room and Mr Hale's study, and her plan allows Margaret and Mrs Hale to join the conversation between Mr Hale and Thornton. Thus, the house in Crampton, the suburb of Milton, is not restricted by the segregation of gender. According to Carolyn Lambert, "Mr Hale's unconventional gendering is balanced by that of Margaret who is increasingly forced… to make authoritative decisions about where and how the family will live" (89). Indeed, Margaret's involvement in the distribution of the spaces of the house in Crampton contributes to her transgression of gender and class norms in the Victorian age. In contrast to Margaret's tired and wearisome drive in Aunt Shaw's carriage in London, the drive in Milton offers her the incentives of a new, modernised city and an elevated domestic position.

Regarding the funeral of Mrs Hale, in accordance with the norms of the Victorian age, Mr Hale objects to Margaret's demand to attend. According to Davidoff and Hall, "daughters and widows did not attend funerals because women were beginning to be considered too delicate to bear the public rituals of death", and even when they did, "they were advised to follow the practices of nobility and gentry and remain in the church while the actual burial was taking place outside" (408). However, Margaret thinks that it is strange that middle-class women cannot attend funerals owing to their lack of endurance of grief while poor women go and express their grief. Thus, Margaret has a doubt about the middle-class women's restriction from the public space not to reveal "their emotions" and the expressions "overwhelmed with grief" (*NS* 261), challenging the norm of the middle-class in the Victorian age and the boundary of class. Hence, she accompanies her father, who has been a broken man since his wife's death, without expressing her emotion. As their means of transportation to the funeral, Mrs Thornton suggests that the Hales should use their private carriage, which makes Margaret angry even if she does not want Thornton, whose proposal she rejected, to attend. After all, Mr Hale and Margaret travel to the funeral by coach, and she sits "by him in the coach", supports him "in her arms" and repeats "all the noble verses" or "texts" (*NS* 263) that she can remember. Judging from their using the coach, there is some distance between the Hale's home and the place of the funeral ritual and burial. According to Michel Foucault, "the cemetery" is a "strange heterotopia" (1998; 241) whose functions have transformed with the evolution of a society's history. Foucault explains that until the end of the eighteenth century, the cemetery was "placed at the heart of the city, next to the church", which was associated with "real belief in the resurrection of bodies and immortality of the soul" (1998; 241). However, "from the start of the nineteenth century, cemeteries began to be located at the outside of cities,...the suburbs", because of "the bourgeois appropriation" aimed at "the individualisation of death" and separation from "an obsession with death as an illness" (Foucault 1998; 241). While Gaskell does not use the words, "the cemetery and burial", the scene of the funeral service in which "Dixon directed Margaret's notice to Nicholas Higgins and his daughter, standing a little aloof" (*NS* 263) and Thornton "had been present...behind a group of people,...no one recognised him" (264) reveals that the funeral service takes place in the open space of the cemetery in the suburbs. Margaret rejects to use Thornton's private carriage which middle-class people think is proper, choosing to go by coach to the funeral and support Mr Hale during the drive to the remote funeral site, taking over the role of patriarch from her father, who is too broken to pray. Margaret's presence at her mother's funeral service, in the cemetery, represents her spirit of revolt against the middle-class norms of the Victorian era. Indeed, as Foucault argues, the cemetery is a heterotopia where Margaret's transgression of the norms of Victorian middle-class is "represented" and the restriction of the women is "contested" and "inverted" (1998; 239).

After the death of her parents, Margaret visits Helstone with Mr Bell by train and the fly—a rental carriage common in the Victorian era. When she is on the train bound for the south, she enjoys the pastoral and calm scenery from the window of it, having a comfort and romantic "waking dream" (*NS* 376). She remembers "German Idyls—of Herman and Dorothea—of Evangeline" (*NS* 376).Wendy Parkins argues that "there is a self-consciousness in the narrative voice in juxtaposing disparate signifiers and allusions" to "the pastoral in Goethe and Longfellow" (2004; 511); however, I think that Margaret imagines herself to be a refugee from the French Revolution in Goethe's poem—an exile from the modernised world to the old one, or a vagabond who seeks for her lover in the primaeval forest. As she is tired from her life in the modernised industrial city and her displacement in London, the tranquil scenery of one farm after another seen from the window of the train lets her feel calm and have a transient repose. However, the journey on the fly makes her feel "ineffable longing" (*NS* 376) and a lonesome feeling that she is alone and an orphan. The unvarying scenery of Helstone hurts her, and she is shocked by the contrast between her changed circumstances and the changeless nature of Helstone. She looks back with nostalgia on the days when she was with her parents, as she feels: "Every mile was redolent of association, which she would not have missed for the world" (*NS* 376). She feels sentimental, as Helstone's landscape makes her aware of her parents' passing. In contrast to the scenery from the window of the train which passes faster than the coach, the sight from the fly makes her feel close to memory of her parents and notice that nature does not change while her circumstances have changed. Thus, while her journey home by rail provides comfort for her, the drive on the fly carriage makes her uneasy and recognise the contrast between the fragility and transience of human life and unchangeable nature.

Informed of Mr Bell's serious illness, Margaret decides to go to Oxford by herself. As Mrs Shaws and Edith object to Margaret travelling unaccompanied on a train, Margaret misses her train and becomes irritated. Even after "various discussions on propriety and impropriety" (*NS* 400), Margaret does not change her decision to go see Mr Bell, and eventually, she is accompanied by Captain Lennox on her journey to Oxford on the next train. This scene demonstrates that a woman traveling alone by train was considered dangerous within the middle-class gender ideology. On the train to Oxford, Margaret is "surprised herself at the firmness with which she asserted something of her right to independence of action" (*NS* 400). While she feels her body weakened by recent tragedies, she recognises the resolve of her inner decision and strong desire for independence. Her satisfaction and comfort in a railway carriage, caused by her departure from Harley Street, reveal that she has become confident in her mobility and decision. While the railroad used to be the source of loneliness and uneasiness during her journeys to and from Helstone, her decision to go to Oxford by rail demonstrates that she has become accustomed to the modernised transportation and aware of her inclination for independence.

The advent of railroad networks offers Margaret and the other characters in *North and South* a different space from those in *Jane Eyre* and *Villette*. The former represents Margaret's involvement in technological developments and the capitalist modernity. The railway network allows her and the other characters the opportunity to travel long distances and have frequent and fast mobility. This, in turn, prompts them to overcome the boundaries of regions and become entangled in modernity and change; however, it also becomes the source of their anxiety and uneasiness, which are byproducts of modernity.

CHAPTER 3
Transformation and Identity

Wendy Parkins argues that "a certain degree of mobility and change is inevitable in modern life" (2004; 513). The mobile protagonists in *Jane Eyre*, *Villette* and *North and South* undergo changes as they experience displacement, negotiate with society, and produce their space. All three novels begin with descriptions of the protagonists' dependent life in wealthy relatives' houses, and due to their marginal situations, Jane Eyre, Lucy Snowe and Margaret Hale voluntarily or involuntarily confine themselves in liminal space and try to accept an ambiguous identity. This chapter explores how they transform themselves through mobility and clarifies how their mobility and travel produce identity. Tim Cresswell's argument that identities are built and achieved through mobility suggests that mobility provides the protagonists, who are suffering from their displacement, with the possibility of challenging their marginalised position and trying to build their own identity in the new circumstances. Anthony Giddens argues that "the body" is not only "a physical entity", but also "an action-system, a mode of praxis", and "its practical immersion in the interactions of day-to-day life is an essential part of the sustaining of a coherent sense of self-identity" (Giddens 99). His argument also suggests that, as the most basic action in daily life, walking offers the protagonists the space and time to sustain or discover a sense of self-identity. Thus, based on these recent arguments, this chapter explores the relationship of the middle-class women's literary space, mobility, walking, identity, and modernity.

According to Andrea Kaston Tange, "British middle-class identity from the 1830s to the 1870s was clearly architectural" and "the way house was designed to distribute people through space helped establish the personal and social identities of everyone who entered" (6). By placing static, immovable "walls", Victorian middle-class people tried to accommodate and control the interactions of the occupants of the house to segregate them in accordance with "class- and gender-based expectations" (Tange 17). Tange's argument helps to analyse the interplay between the heroines of the selected novels and domestic spaces they experience through their mobility. Although the Victorians tended to associate one space with a single identity, as Tange argues, there are some spaces that are not identified as a particular person's privilege or identity. More importantly, Jane, Lucy, and Margaret's frequent violation of the rules of spatial usage blurs a spatial division built upon the Victorian culture, that between the public and the private, between inside and outside. Based on these sociological, geographical, and cultural theories, this chapter explores how the protagonists negotiate with the Victorian spatial norms through their mobility and produce their own identities. In this chapter, I also examine the heterotopic spaces, which were not addressed in the previous chapters. These spaces often facilitate the self-discovery and the discovery of the hidden self of the heroines in the three novels. Illustrating the heroines' experience of spatial ambiguity and transgression, I demonstrate that *Jane Eyre*, *Villette*, and *North and South* reflect the complex identity of middle-class women within modernity.

3.1. *Jane Eyre*

Jane's marginalised situation makes it difficult for her to develop a sympathetic relationship with the Reeds. John Reed blames her for being a dependent with no money—almost a beggar—and claims that she should not "live here with gentlemen's children like us" (*JE* 13). Even Bessie, the servant admired by Jane, arbitrarily regards her position as "less than a servant" (*JE* 15) because she does not earn her living. Susan Fraiman says that Jane's social ambiguity is a kind of "legacy" inherited from her parents, who were situated between the two classes (616). Though the education of Jane's father, a poor clergyman, helped him to elevate himself slightly from the masses of poor people, her mother's marriage lowered her from the class she had been born into. Although the servants know that Jane's father, a poor clergyman, and her mother, Mr Reed's sister, died of typhus a year into their marriage, which was not approved of by grandfather Reed, they admonish Jane to obey the Reed family, especially John—the future master—by persuading her that she is not the Reeds' equal. Jane's marginality makes her unable to share the domestic space with the Reeds. When we meet her for the first time, Jane retreats herself from "the drawing-room" where the Reed family performs the role of the "perfectly happy" (*JE* 9) family drama near the hearth; feeling completely isolated, she miserably enters the breakfast room next to the drawing room. The setting of this scene within the Victorian drawing room or the parlour is significant as these became a newly significant space in both middle-class practical life and fiction. According to Andrea Kaston Tange, "the Victorian drawing-room was the quintessential feminized space within the home" as it was "the place in which women spent most of their days"; here, women were engaged in "letter writing, plain or decorative sewing, reading, visiting, conversation, going over household accounts, interviewing servants, or undertaking the many other tasks that might occupy their time" (62). However, the drawing room "was not only a private space" but it was also a space where "women's actions" were foregrounded and their "accomplishments were expected to be on display... in order to confirm the respectability and the status of the family" (Tange 63). In Gateshead Hall, the drawing room is where Mrs Reed performs her "feminine authority" as a mistress by excluding the dangerous outsider—Jane. Jane finds that "a more marked line of separation" (*JE* 33) has been drawn between her and the Reed family and that her entry into the drawing room has become more strictly regulated after she attacks John like a fierce animal. Jane is assigned "a small closet" (*JE* 33) to sleep in and eat alone, and even during the Christmas season, she has to spend her time alone in "the solitary and silent nursery", excluded from "every enjoyment" (*JE* 34–35). According to Tange, the Victorian nursery was located at the top of the house, being "far removed from the rest of the house" as children "were not yet sanctioned to appear throughout the house as fully integrated members of the middle class" (24). Children had to learn bourgeois values, norms, and behaviours from their parents to become "'respectable' members of the middle-class community", and it was in the dining room and the drawing room "in which the middle-class family's identity was most prominently on display" (Tange 24). While Eliza, John, and Georgiana are frequently summoned to these central rooms in Gateshead Hall, Jane is "restricted so long to the nursery" that the dining room and the drawing room become "awful regions" (*JE* 38) for her. This means that Jane is not recognised as a member of a middle-class family and has no opportunities to learn middle-class norms and values. While Bessie often employs Jane as "a sort of under nursery-maid" (*JE* 37) to tidy the room, she is not welcome at the servants' apartments or the kitchen where they enjoy gathering. Child Jane without family and money is "a heterogeneous thing" (*JE* 19) and "an uncongenial alien" (20) who belongs to none of the groups occupying the middle-class house. Being a member of neither the middle-class family nor their employees, she is kept "at a distance" (*JE* 11) from others and is miserably placeless. Spending time alone as per her aunt's order, child Jane "felt an instinctive certainty that she [Mrs Reed] would no longer endure me under the same roof with her" (*JE* 33).

According to Hoeveveler, "the red-room" where Jane is confined as punishment for revelling against her future master, John, "figures as the first of many enclosed spaces that the heroine has to rewrite in order to script herself out of the limitations imposed on her" (209). As pointed out by several critics, the red-room is a gothic space that contains the death bed of her uncle, a wardrobe with Mrs Reed's secret parchments and jewels, and a great looking-glass. Confined in the red-room as punishment for her struggle with John Reed, Jane is frightened by the gloomy and chill atmosphere of the room. She later becomes involuntarily fascinated by the mirror between the wardrobe and the window:

> All looked colder and darker in that visionary hollow than in reality: and the strange little figure there gazing at me, with a white face and arms specking the gloom, and glittering the eyes of fear moving where all else was tiny phantoms, half fairy, half imp... before the eyes of the belated travellers. (*JE* 18)

Jane recognises the potential of the mysterious space the mirror offers her and is conscious that the figure reflected in the mirror is distinct from the figure in reality. According to Michel Foucault, as we can see ourselves in the mirror—where we are absent—the mirror is a utopia; however, the mirror is also a "heterotopia" as it exists in reality, where it exerts a kind of "counteraction" (1998; 240) on the position we occupy. Brontë utilises the mirror—the heterotopic space—to depict the protagonist's true nature behind her appearance. Jane's true figure, which appears as a "counteraction", does not represent a girl who is terrified at her confinement but a "revolted slave" (*JE* 18) with a fierce look akin to phantoms, fairies, and imps. As Julian Wolfreys argues, the phantom or "ghost" is the "transgressive figure par excellence" (111), as it returns from the dead to haunt the living. According to Wolfreys, "transgression" means "to step over or beyond a limit or boundary, to cross a threshold, to move beyond the commonly determined bounds (of law, decency, or whatever)" (3); and thus, since the phantom or ghost commits the ultimate transgression (between the boundaries of the dead and living) it is the "transgressive figure par excellence" (111). The transgressive scene where Jane supposes that she saw the ghost of the dead Mr Reed is related to her conception of herself in the mirror as a phantom. That is, Jane's confinement in the red-room for her transgressive behaviours of struggling "like a mad cat" (*JE* 34) with John Reed transforms her into a transgressive child-like phantom. Her transgressive conjecture that she saw the ghost of her dead uncle arises from her fearful recognition that her existence within the middle-class house is transgressive. According to Wolfreys, for the Victorians "to be modern meant to remember, and to suffer passively the haunting effects of the past, lest that past, in having been forgotten, return to transgress and haunt one's self...all the more violently" (124). Thus, throughout the narrative, Jane remembers the haunting appearance of her dead uncle in the red-room, which is part of the modern world. Consequently, she is sent to Lowood Institution, whose aims are hardship, patience, and self-denying, to control her transgressive actions and imagination.

In contrast to her spoiled cousins, ten-year-old Jane is an avid reader and devotes herself to reading the books, such as Bewick's History of British Birds, History of Rome, and Gulliver's Travels, which are brought out of the library by Bessie during the Reeds' absence. As Hoeveler points out, reading provides Jane with "the power of the logos, the word" (190), interest in the world, and the wisdom to live. However, "her verbal power" makes Mrs Reed consider her as a "dangerous duplicity" (*JE* 22) and leads Jane to a heated discussion with Mrs Reed; "What would Uncle Reed say to you, if he were alive?" (34). Jane's expulsion from Gateshead to the Lowood Institution results from both the improper language she uses with her aunt and her vivid account of her miserable life to the apothecary. Jane's eloquent speech, which incorporated Helen Burn's "warnings against the indulgence of resentment", rids Miss Temple of her misunderstanding that Jane is a liar, as Mr Brocklehurst had suggested (*JE* 84). Helen Burns, a book-lover akin to Jane, inspires her to learn harder when Miss Temple bids Helen to read a page of Virgil; "Helen obeyed, my organ of veneration expanding at every sounding line" (*JE* 87). While Jane does not understand the Latin phrases, she is so excited by Helen's deep knowledge that she respects her and hates Miss Scatcherd, who abuses Helen. Similar to how she claimed, "unjust!" (*JE* 19) in the red-room, Jane evokes fury and rebellion against Miss Scatcherd's unjust treatment of Helen, who is calm, resigned, and enduring silently. Helen, a fourteen-year-old girl abandoned by her father, longs for her old home in

Northumberland, where her father lives with his new wife, and yearns for the true home in heaven, where she believes that God awaits her. As Sandra M. Gilbert and Susan Gubar point out, Miss Temple and Helen are like "mothers for Jane" (346), who listen to her story, comfort her, and lead her to regulate her temper. Like her name, Miss Temple is kind and angelic and has a sacred nature with dignified strength. She watches over Jane quietly without interfering to ensure that she does not cross the boundaries of the restrictions and rules of the school. Jane abides by Miss Temple's precepts and the lessons and assimilates her "settled feeling" (*JE* 100), becoming a teacher after six years of education by overcoming her rebellious spirit and transgressive actions during Miss Temple's tenure at Lowood.

However, when eighteen-year-old Jane is separated from Miss Temple, who leaves Lowood Institution for her marriage, she acknowledges that "I was no longer the same" (*JE* 100). Walking about in her room, she discovers a new thought occurring in her interior:

> [A]nother discovery dawned on me—namely, that in the interval I had undergone a transforming process; that my mind had put off all it had borrowed of Miss Temple—or rather, that she had taken with her the serene atmosphere I had been breathing in her vicinity—and that now I was left in my natural element, and beginning to feel the stirring of old emotions. (*JE* 101)

Jane is aware that her feeling has been released from Miss Temple's serene oppression and that she has changed. While she admires Miss Temple very much, as Gilbert and Gubar claim, Jane does not choose "Miss Temple's way of ladylike repression, nor Helen's way of saintly renunciation" (347) to confront the world; instead, she challenges society with her curiosity and rebellious spirit. After Miss temple's departure, Jane's impression of Lowood is transformed from her home into that of a "prison-ground, exile limits", and she desires to be free from the confinement "within their boundaries" (*JE* 101). The letter from Mrs Fairfax, the manager of Thornfield Hall, initiates a new phase of Jane's life to be a governess at Thornfield. The location of Thornfield, "seventy miles nearer London" than the remote country where Lowood is situated, is "a recommendation" (*JE* 105) to her. Jane yearns to go to a place that has "life and movement" and states: "Millcote was a large manufacturing town on the banks of the A—; a busy place doubtless: so much the better; it would be a complete change at least" (*JE* 105). Bored by Lowood's rules and systems and eight years of isolation from society, Jane desires "a complete change" (*JE* 105) in her life, place, and occupation.

While Jane evaluates Thornfield to be closer to London—the metropolitan city—she does not necessarily prefer a manufacturing town like Millcote over the rural area. As she is not fascinated by "the idea of long chimneys and clouds of smoke" (*JE* 105), the symbol of manufacturing and capitalism, her sensitivity is not always oriented towards modernity. Furthermore, she knows that her father, a clergyman, died of typhus contracted from the poor in a manufacturing town. Thus, she is not always interested in the industrial city, which is associated with modernity. Her longing is for change, movement, and liberty, and her excitement spurred by this change allows her to reveal the transgressive movement; "in the lobby, where I was wandering like a troubled spirit". Thus, her original nature, "like a troubled spirit" (*JE* 107), which Miss Temple at Lowood attempts to reform, is again brought out. However, when she leaves Lowood with the trunk she had brought with her eight years previously, she is no longer the same person and has become "genteel enough" (*JE* 108). Having acquired the skills necessary for a governess and teacher, such as knowledge in English, French, drawing, and music, Jane has confidence in her ability; moreover, she is informed by Bessie of Mr Eyre's, her father's brother and a person equivalent in status to the Reeds, visit to Gateshead, and his journey to Madeira, an island in the North Atlantic Ocean. Thus, Jane, who has suffered from displacement since her childhood, becomes confident from knowing that she has a gentlemanly uncle who has worried about her despite his remoteness. Jane learns that her uncle is crossing the boundaries of nations to voyage to a different country, just as she considers leaving the boundary of Lowood. Modernity has no geographical boundaries (Berman 15); the parallel drawn by Brontë between Jane and her uncle's actions of going out to the new world brings both of them into the space of modernity.

Her earnest desire for incidents, animation and passion for life awakened as soon as she becomes accustomed to the quiet life at Thornfield Hall can be attributed to her "restlessness" (*JE* 129). When she raises the trap-door of the attic and looks out over the quiet field, she longs for "the busy world, towns, regions full of life" (*JE* 129) and more opportunities for discourse with various kinds of people. Thus, she yearns for the modernised world outside Thornfield and feels confined. However, remaining constrained, she confesses that "my sole relief was to walk along the corridor of the third storey, backwards and forwards, safe in the silence and solitude of the spot" (*JE* 129). Her solitary walks along the corridors of the third storey, away from the other residents like Mrs Fairfax, Adel, and a nurse, would have been considered strange or transgressive actions for a governess to undertake. Walking along the gloomy corridor like that of "Bluebeard's castle" (*JE* 126), Jane proudly locates the door where the tragic and preternatural laugh is issued from. However, her ramblings in the third storey are abandoned when Rochester remarks that she is only "a curious sort of bird through the close-set bars of a cage" and "a vivid, restless, resolute captive" (*JE* 162) in the cage. Rochester is aware of Jane's walks in the third storey, where his secret and history are hidden. It seems that he is cautious about her transgression, as she is a woman who insists that "it is narrow-minded in their more privileged fellow-creatures to say that they (women) ought to confine themselves" (*JE* 130) in the house, and who challenges and criticises the order which has been maintained by the middle-class and aristocratic men. According to Kate Fergason Ellis, "mobility is a defining condition of (male) bourgeois subjectivity shaping, and being shaped by, the bourgeois revolution" (172). Jane is a mobile woman whom the male bourgeois have to control to ensure that she does not cross the boundaries of patriarchal norms.

Jane's first experience of marginalisation in Thornfield arises in the scene of her conversation with Rochester. According to Linda McDowell, "marginalization" is "the exclusion of certain people from useful participation in society" (178). Summoned to the dining room by Rochester, Jane is requested to speak something to please him. According to Andrea Kaston Tange, the dining room, which displays the male owner's taste in wine, "was associated with masculinity" (138). The "absurd" and "insolent" (*JE* 156) utterances of Rochester, who is drunk on wine, that she should respect him because he is as old as her father and has had lots of experiences abroad, impose his patriarchal oppression on Jane. Jane's response that these reasons do not serve as his superiority: "your claim to superiority depends on the use you have made of your time and experience" (*JE* 157) surprises him. Her power of words challenges his patriarchy. Jane's insistence that nobody who is "free-born" would submit to a master's "insolence" even "for a salary" (*JE* 158) displeases Rochester. He warns her that a "raw schoolgirl-governess" should not "venture on generalities of which she is intensely ignorant" (*JE* 158). Thus, while considering her to have the marginalised existence of a governess, he admits that she has the intelligence to subvert and challenge class norms, as well as goodness and a stainless personality like a "nonnette (nun)" (*JE* 154). Confessing that he is only a sinner produced by the circumstances where rich young gentlemen are prone to succumb to the depraved life, Rochester notices her intense ability to listen. In Thornfield, Jane utilises both her ability to speak and also to listen.

Jane's marginalisation at Thornfield is also highlighted when Rochester's guests are invited to the house. Jane states that she would like to confine herself to "my sanctum of the schoolroom" during their stay because she thinks that it becomes "a very pleasant refuge in time of trouble" (*JE* 193). Even when she goes down to get something to eat for Adele, she seeks "a back-stairs which conducted directly to the kitchen" (*JE* 194) to avoid encountering the guests. When Adele is tired of staying in the schoolroom, Jane takes her out into "the gallery", and they sit down "on the top step of the stairs" (*JE* 196) to listen to the sound of the music issuing out of the piano from the drawing-room. According to Tange, "the liminal spaces of the middle-class home—staircases, halls, and corridors" offered "spatial possibilities for complicating the hierarchies of gender- and class-based identities" (177). As she is not a servant, Jane is not expected to use the backstairs.

As Tange points out, "the Victorian governess—a figure whose position was explicitly that of paid labourer within the home, but whose qualification for the task was ideally that she had grown up as a privileged daughter in a middle-class household" (Tange 178). Indeed, when requested to accompany Adele into the drawing room by Rochester the next evening, Jane recognises that most of the guests ignore her as she is a governess and hears some of them, such as Lady Ingram and her daughter, Blanche, speak ill of their governess. Jane hears Blanche reproach the governess for being a "nuisance" (*JE* 205). Jane's dislocation as a governess in Thornfield is highlighted when she, hidden behind the window curtain between the drawing room and the dining room, observes them. When Rochester and his guests begin playing charades, a sort of pantomime, in the drawing room, Jane is marginalised by them and hears Lady Ingham's negative remark about Jane: "she looks too stupid for any game of the sort" (*JE* 212). Although Jane sees that the first act, where Rochester and Miss Ingham portray a marriage ceremony, predicts their marriage, she is convinced that Miss Ingham's pride and self-complacency will fail to gain his love. However, the thought that he might marry Miss Ingham because "her rank and connections suited him" (*JE* 216) makes Jane nervous. While she considers Rochester a man unlikely to be affected by such commonplace motives when choosing his wife, she recognises that his entire class was instilled from childhood with these principles and ideas. Admitting the difference of position between Rochester and herself, Jane thinks that she cannot blame him or Miss Ingham for cherishing their principles and that they must have reasons that she cannot presume. Thus, Jane does not always transgress the social norms based on class in the Victorian era, even if she claims that Miss Ingham is not worthy of Rochester.

According to Marshall Berman, "modern environments and experiences cut across all boundaries of geography and ethnicity, of class and nationality, of religion and ideology" (15). Although Jane crosses the boundary of class when she insists that anybody born free does not have to submit themselves to a master's insolence, she now recoils from the idea of modernity.

Rochester's proposal offers Jane the opportunity to elevate her status. However, as her love for him transforms her into a vulnerable woman, she confesses the following:

> My future husband was becoming to me my whole world; and more than the world: almost my hope of heaven. He stood between me and every thought of religion, as an eclipse intervenes between man and the broad sun. I could not, in those days, see God for His creature: of whom I had made an idol. (*JE* 316)

As Carol Senf suggests, Jane has almost lost her "sense of self" (144), and she cannot see even God, her belief. Even though she tries to control her future husband, his power over her oppresses her as she has no family connections or money. Moreover, as he is as old as her father, he can easily exert his patriarchal power on her. Discovering the existence of his secret wife, Jane is temporarily confused, due to Rochester's offer to take her to a villa on the shores of the Mediterranean and his explanation that he married Bertha—his first wife—only because he was ordered to do so by his father. However, she is inspired by her innate self-confidence, courage, and sense of justice to leave Thornfield, which she had come to think of as her home. Nevertheless, she is forced to leave as a nobody—she is no longer a student or a governess. While

Jane realises that she would experience social marginalisation for being penniless, begging, displaced, and homeless, she is exempt from being reduced to his mistress and the ethical transgression it entails. Her resolution is revealed through the following statement:

> 'I care for myself. The more solitary, the more friendless, the more unsustained I am, the more I will respect myself. I will keep the law given by God; sanctioned by man. I will hold to the principles received by me when I was sane, and not mad—as I am now.' (*JE* 365)

Thus, Jane is determined to observe "laws and principles", however strict they are, and considers that they should be "inviolate", especially when there is "temptation" (*JE* 365). Overcoming temptation, Jane regains her self-confidence and "her sense of self" and is ready to escape the confinement of Thornfield through "drear flight and homeless wandering" (*JE* 369). She chooses to live as a solitary vagrant, who embraces the sanctity of her person, rather than live as Rochester's mistress who is reconciled to a life like "a temporary heaven" (*JE* 368), even though both positions lead to her marginalisation. Since her self-respect, self-confidence, and self-control enable her to overcome the temptation, she is exempted from the moral and ethical transgression.

Jane's wandering in Whitcross represents a transgressive movement, and as Charlotte Mathieson argues, it moves "beyond the appropriate social order of female mobility" (55). Indeed, Jane thinks it "impossible" that the inmates of Moor House would sympathise with "her own wretched position" (*JE* 384). When she is eventually invited to Moor House by the Rivers family after three days of roaming, Jane gives them an alias, which demonstrates that Jane feels ashamed of degrading herself by having acted like a mendicant and is anxious about being discovered by Rochester. Crossing the threshold of the house, she feels relieved to know that she is "no longer outcast, vagrant, and disowned by the wide world" (*JE* 387). According to Mathieson, Jane is "cast out from the space of the nation" (53); it is only when she enters the threshold of Moor House that she returns to the map of the nation. Jane, acknowledging that her wandering was a transgressive behaviour from the norms of feminine decency, does not inform Rochester of it when they later meet. Resuming her "natural manner and character" (*JE* 387), Jane is treated as "a visitor" in "the parlour" (395) by Diana Rivers, and Jane feels pleasure in yielding to the authority radiated by her looks and speech. Thus, Jane has to separate herself from the transgression to recover her feminine decency as a middle-class woman. The Rivers siblings recognise Jane as an educated person and "some young lady" (*JE* 390) who has injudiciously left her friends. Jane notices a "perfect congeniality of tastes, sentiments, and principles" (*JE* 402) between Jane and the sisters. As they love Moor House, their "sequestered home", Jane comes to find "a charm both potent and permanent" in the "small and antique structure" of the house (*JE* 402). She, like the sisters, comes to cling to not only the house but also the landscapes of the purple moors surrounding their residence "with a perfect enthusiasm of attachment", sharing "both its strength and truth" (*JE* 402). Jane comprehends "the fascination of the locality" and "the consecration of its loneliness" (*JE* 402). The details of the pastoral scenery bring her "so many pure and sweet sources of pleasure" (*JE* 403). While she yearned for town life in Lowood Institution, her encounter with Diana and Mary changes her attitude, and the sisters' home, which is sequestered from society and surrounded by nature, becomes Jane's ideal. Even though her affection for the sisters changes her taste, Jane appears to invoke her innate taste for quiet, modest, and secluded pastoral life rather than town life. She is represented as being uncomfortable in the industrial and busy city during her visit to Millcote with Rochester. While the Lowood Institution faced the typhus epidemic, she spent her time walking in the woods. Jane is entranced with the charm of the region with its local features and loves Moor House as much as it is loved by the Rivers sisters. This love for the sequestered home in the country connotes that she will finally choose Rochester's manor-house of Ferndean as her residence.

In contrast to the Rivers sisters' and Jane's love for Moor House, Jane supposes that "Nature was not to St John that treasury of delight it was to his sisters" and that he does not roam the moors to enjoy their soothing silence by seeking out or dwelling on 'the thousand peaceful delights they could yield" (*JE* 404). St John self-deprecatingly remarks that he is only "the incumbent of a poor country parish" (*JE* 400) despite possessing the Rivers name, and thinks that it would be terrible for his sisters to become governesses. He is not content with his country house in the morass and ascribes his poverty to his father's debt, which was brought about by speculations he undertook following John Eyre's advice. Jane's congruence with Diana and Mary is later revealed to be linked to their kinship, as St John later informs Jane that John Eyre—her uncle—is the brother of Mrs Rivers—his mother. Thus, Jane and the Rivers siblings prove to be cousins, and Jane is no longer a visitor for the Rivers siblings but a member of their family. She states that she has not considered the Reeds to be her relatives and that the first connection she has established with her extended family has been with the Rivers. While Jane's indifference to her huge inheritance from her uncle—John Eyre—surprises St John, Jane's acquisition of her fortune is important to developing the narrative and her recognising her identity. It allows her to share the inheritance with the Rivers siblings, learn domestic accomplishments from the sisters in Moor House, and build an economically equal relationship with Rochester.

St John establishes a small cottage and a school for girls in the village and offers Jane the position of the schoolmistress. Jane's acceptance of this position transforms her into an independent woman. Jane, who previously had to rely on others to live, becomes a teacher for the girls in the village and attains economic independence. Jane is content with the cottage, even though it is modest and is located half a mile from the village—Morton. It is also "a safe asylum" for Jane, who experienced "the fear of servitude with strangers" (*JE* 408) during her stint as the governess in the rich house. Moreover, this also causes a significant change in Jane's character as she overcomes her prejudice against the cottagers' children or farmers' daughters and her bias against the poor in the village. Initially, struggling to understand their broad accent, roughness and ignorance, she considers teaching them as a "degraded" (*JE* 414) vocation; however, she soon reflects on her bias and realises that some of the rustic girls among the children are sharp-witted and desirous of information and improvement. According to Carol Senf, "this cottage is also the space where she learns compassion for other poor people and sees them not only as metaphors of her own condition but as unique individuals" (148). I think that Jane learns to view people with humility, without bias and estimates them as individuals with distinct personalities and possibilities rather than as "metaphors of her own condition". Jane originally assesses the value of an individual not by their family connections and economic state but by personality and faculty. For example, she claims that "I have as much soul as you—and full as much heart!...we stood at God's feet, equal—as we are!" (*JE* 292) to Rochester; this demonstrates Jane's recognition that human beings should not be assessed by their station, wealth, or appearance, but by their soul, faculty, and intelligence. Jane, who suffered marginalisation amongst the wealthy, regrets having looked down on the cottagers and farmers for being uneducated. After becoming a teacher, she often accepted invitations from her pupils' parents to visit their homes and found these experiences pleasant; she also relished being a favourite in the neighbourhood. However, when she describes that living among "general regard, though it be but the regard of working people" is like "sitting in sunshine, calm and sweet" (*JE* 423), we can continue to see traces of her disdain for the working people in the village. In contrast to Margaret's sympathy for the working people, Jane's acquaintanceship with them is temporary and rather self-centred. Similarly, as soon as she learns of her inheritance from John Eyre—her uncle who made a fortune from the wine trade in Madeira—she abandons the teaching position at the girl's school. While Jane is not interested in the commerce of the capitalist world market, she indirectly benefits from her uncle's involvement in the capitalist world market and becomes a rich woman possessing twenty thousand pounds. Perry Anderson construes Marshall Berman's modernity, which consists of two elements: "economic development", which refers to "the gigantic objective transformations of society unleashed by the capitalist world market"; and "self-development", which refers to "the momentous subjective transformations of individual life and personality, which occur under their impact" (98). Upon receiving the large inheritance from her uncle, Jane calls back Diana and Mary, who have been working as governesses in southern towns, and shares her inheritance with her three cousins equally. She thinks that "justice would be done" (*JE* 445): the Rivers siblings regain what their father lost due to his false speculation undertaken under the recommendation of John Eyre. Thus, Jane serves as an agent for the dead John Eyre, who never forgave the father of the Rivers siblings following a quarrel. Recognising that the Rivers family's economic hardship pushes them to the verge of closing up their home, Jane resolves that she will attach herself for life to Diana and Mary in Moor House. Jane's renovation and innovation of Moor House by using her inheritance demonstrates that she has both the accomplishments of a middle-class lady and economic independence. When she claims that "I want to enjoy my own faculties as well as to cultivate those of other people" (*JE* 450), she is conscious of her self-identity as a middle-class woman who cares about domestic details in the house. Jane does not forget to pay special care to Diana and Mary's sentiments regarding the renovation: "the ordinary sitting-rooms I left much as they were: for I knew Diana and Mary would derive more pleasure from seeing again the old homely tables, and chairs, and beds, than from the spectacle of the smartest innovations" (*JE* 452). To please them, she is happy to arrange "dark handsome carpets and curtains" and "some carefully selected antique ornaments in porcelain and bronze, new coverings, and mirrors, and dressing cases...they looked fresh without being glaring" (*JE* 452). According to Tange, "a good middle-class home was expected at all times to reflect the 'character' of its occupants, whose behaviour and possessions marked them as respectable" (18). Tange also argues that "the Victorian desire to preserve a sense of middle-class privilege most often relied upon the assumption that taste could not be learned but merely would be effortlessly displayed in the daily actions of those who were 'truly' middle-class" (18). At Moor House Jane regains the privileged sensibilities of a middle-class woman. When the cleaning and arrangement of the furniture are over, Jane considers Moor House as "a model of bright modest snugness within" (*JE* 452). Thus, Moor House serves as a proving ground for Jane to recover her domesticity before returning to Rochester's residence. Moor House is transformed into a more comfortable home for Jane, Diana and Mary. However, St John's cool response disappoints Jane, and his proposal to her to be a missionary wife in India tortures her. She rejects his proposal by saying, "if I join St John, I abandon half myself" (*JE* 466); that is, she feels that if she married him to go to India, she would give up her identity. She conceives that she no more loves him than he loves her. Moreover, she regains her decency as a middle-class woman at Moor House and does not succumb to the transgressive behaviours. When he threatens her by stating the following, "Refuse to be my wife, and you limit yourself forever to a track of selfish ease and barren obscurity" (*JE* 471), she considers that "as a man, he would have wished to coerce me into obedience" (472). Discovering that St John is a man who adheres to patriarchy rather than the spirit of a clergyman, she recognises his imperfection, realises that his nature is equivalent to hers, and finds the courage to "resist" him (*JE* 469) by continuing to reject his proposal. She realises that even if she must leave for India with him as his missionary assistant or "a useful tool" (*JE* 479), she has to find out what had become of Rochester before leaving. Thus, Moor House, Jane's ideal home as a place of security and concord, is transformed into a place of danger and suspicion because of St John's patriarchal oppression.

Jane feels like "the messenger-pigeon flying home" (*JE* 487) while she drives to Thornfield by coach. Although she had decided that she would never return when leaving there a year previously, her reference to a pigeon, which has homing instinct, signifies that she considers Thornfield—Rochester's residence—her true home. As she walks toward Thornfield Hall, her heart becomes filled with nostalgia: "How fast I walked! How I ran sometimes! How I looked forward to catching the first view of the well-known woods! With what feelings I welcomed single trees I knew, and familiar glimpses of meadow and hill between them!" (*JE* 488) The marked exclamatory tone of these sentences palpably conveys Jane's longing for Thornfield. However, instead of a stately house, Jane sees a blackened ruin; "The front was, as I had once seen it in a dream, but a shell-like wall, very high and very fragile-looking, perforated with paneless windows: no roof, no battlements, no chimneys—all had crashed in" (*JE* 489). The ruined building connotes the change in Rochester, who has become blind and crippled because of the fire set by his mad wife—Bertha; the shell-like wall represents Rochester's blind eye, and the lack of battlements indicates his lost hand. The symbol of Rochester's materialism, power and secret is destroyed, and Bertha's suicide provides Jane with her victory and liberation. According to Dianne Long Hoeveler, "the excessive…body of Bertha confronts the…repressed body of Jane as the two women struggle for possession of the men and his estates" (216), and "Bertha has always represented a split-off element or component within Jane's own psyche" (220). Indeed, Jane overcomes her innate transgressive nature, which is shared by Bertha as well; however, I do not agree that Jane has aspired for Rochester's property, for her disregard for wealth, materialism and urban life is proved by her willingness to share her inheritance with her cousins and her affection for the sequestered Moor House.

Jane's last destination is the manor-house of Ferndean, which is about thirty miles away from Thornfield. Discovering the blinded Rochester leaning over the grate in the gloomy drawing room, she does not feel fear at the sight of "that sightless Samson" (*JE* 498). Rochester, who has lost his sight and left hand, is no longer a proud masculine man and is transformed into a feminised man confined to the drawing room. Finding Rochester to be a weakened, tamed, feminised man confined to the house, she finds "her own faculty" (*JE* 450) to take care of him. Having the servant clean the parlour and prepare a comfortable repast for him on arriving at Ferndean Manor, Jane acts as if she were the mistress of the house. Regretting that he was once proud of his strength, Rochester, who now has to depend on foreign guidance, admits his powerlessness to her; in contrast, over the intervening year, Jane has become an independent woman who has regained her station through her family connection to the Rivers and a large inheritance from her uncle. Thus, Jane and Rochester are now equals in reality. She argues that "we are precisely suited in character—perfect concord is the result" (*JE* 519). Ferndean Manor is an estate purchased by Rochester's father for the sake of the game covers. The building is "a considerable antiquity, moderate size, and no architectural pretensions, deep buried in a wood" (*JE* 496). Due to "its ineligible and insalubrious site", Ferndean has remained for a long time "uninhabited and unfurnished" (*JE* 496). Indeed, Ferndean Manor is similar to Moor House; both locations are sequestered from society and surrounded by nature. Similarly, the former is described as an antiquity that has a moderate-sized structure, which is scarcely "distinguishable from the trees; so dank and green were its decaying walls", and has "no flowers no garden-beds" (*JE* 497), while the latter is described as a "gray, small, antique structure" surrounded by "aged firs" and "yew and holly" (*JE* 402), and as having flowers only of the hardiest species. Although Gilbert and Gubar suggest that "its [Ferndean's] valley-of-the-shadow quality makes it seem rather like a Lowood" (369), I argue that Ferndean Manor is more similar to Moor House—the pastoral house. Based on Rochester's confession that his conscience prevented him from confining Bertha to Ferndean Manor because of its dampness, a few critics like Senf have pointed out the unhealthy circumstances of Ferndean (Senf 149). However, the day after Jane and Rochester's reunion, Jane leads him out of the house into some cheerful fields and lets him sit on "a seat for him in a hidden and lovely spot, a dry stump of a tree" and places herself "on his knee" (*JE* 507). As she appreciates "the work of nature" (*JE* 483), she compares him to a vigorous tree and herself to a plant; "You are no ruin, sir—no lightning-struck tree: you are green and vigorous. Plants will grow about your roots, whether you ask them or not, because they take delight in your bountiful shadow" (*JE* 512). Jane seems to believe in the regenerative power of nature. The quiet pastoral home, surrounded by nature and secluded from society, is suitable for Jane and Rochester. According to Kate Ferguson Ellis, "the rural endings of the Radcliffian Gothic move away not only from the industrial economy being created by the bourgeoisie but also from the extremes of the accompanying ideology of separate spheres" (112). The pastoral ending in *Jane Eyre* seems to follow that of the Radcliffian Gothic, and it might also reasonably be argued that the novel ends in the rural setting because of Jane's association of the industrial city with danger, arising from her knowledge that her parents died of typhus contracted from the poor in her father's curacy at a large manufacturing town. Moreover, the open space of Ferndean is free from the patriarchal hierarchy as Jane leads the blinded Rochester as his guide without any restrictions premised on the ideology of separate spheres. While Jane becomes a wealthy woman through her inheritance from John Eyre, who acquired his wealth through commerce in the world market, she is not involved in modernised society or urban life. Her transgressions necessitated by her difficulties are followed by voluntary or involuntary reformations, and on each occasion, she returns to the role of the seemingly docile student, governess, or conventional middle-class woman, who cares about domesticity within the household. Her life with her maimed husband and son in the sequestered rural place is quite private, static, independent from social intervention, and averts the danger, temptation, and ugliness of the economical, industrial, and modernised society. In a sense, she is satisfied with crossing the boundary of class and gender within her own domestic space, as she describes her life with Rochester: "to be together is for us to be at once as free as in solitude, as gay as in company" (*JE* 519). However, she ends her adventures within society and abandons her efforts to cross the threshold of the house or mingle in the public world. Indeed, every time Jane is involved in a transgression, she negotiates with herself rather than society and resolves to confine herself in the domestic sphere to exclude herself from the outer world. However, she cannot always avoid social changes; for example, by assisting her blinded and maimed husband in his work, she will be involved in the public sphere of modernised society. According to Anthony Giddens, "a person's identity is not to be found in behaviour, nor... in the reactions of others, but in the capacity to keep a particular narrative going" (54). Now that Jane has described her biography, she perceives how she has become herself, what she has chosen, and where she is going. Thus, Jane recognises herself as an independent woman who stands aloof from the crowd.

3.2. *Villette*

Among the three protagonists, Lucy Snowe seems to have the most elusive nature. Brontë deliberately veils her heroine's identity by not telling the reader her name and character, and Lucy starts her narrative by describing the house in Bretton, her godmother's house (without even mentioning herself):

> My godmother lived in a handsome house in the clean and ancient town of Bretton. Her husband's family had been there for generations, and bore, indeed, the name of their birthplace—Bretton of Bretton: whether by coincidence, or because some remote ancestor had been a personage of sufficient importance to leave his name to his neighbourhood, I know not. (*V* 5)

As for this opening, Liana F. Piehler argues that the narrator "chooses to introduce her story not with a description, admission, or any other comment about herself, but rather with geographic placement and spatial composition, both forms of definition and closure" (44). However, Lucy's definition and perspective of her godmother's house is very limited, for she "know[s] not" why the Bretton family has the same name as the town. Avoiding the introduction of her own birthplace and home, Lucy does not explain in detail why her godmother invites her—an orphaned child—into her house. Her silence leaves the readers in the dark about the location of the town or the nature of their lives in the house in Bretton, besides Lucy's expression of her satisfaction with the home's cleanliness, quiet peacefulness, and orderliness.

Piehler mentions that Polina Home's arrival and lodging at the Bretton household "finally forces the narrator to identify herself in her own narrative" (45). The arrival of Paulina makes Lucy even more invisible in the house of Bretton; it deprives Lucy of her privileged position "as one child in a household of grown people" (V 5). Consequently, Lucy, who loves to be "a mere looker-on at life" (V 141), willingly engages herself in the role of a calm observer. However, young Lucy finds that Paulina is "an object less conductive to comfort...it was scarcely possible to have before one's eyes" (V 12). Temporarily abandoned by her father, Paulina desperately seeks her father and gradually loses her energy to live; her "signs of home sickness" force the narrator to finally exclaim irritatingly that "I, Lucy Snowe" (V 12) have never experienced home sickness. Following John Graham Bretton's return home, Lucy observes that Paulina stabilises her position in the house by performing as his "silent, diligent, absorbed...gentlewoman" (V 16); she dedicatedly takes care of him, prepares his meals, and confines herself with needlework in the drawing room during his absence. For Lucy, such a young girl's dedication to a grown-up man is "rather absurd" (V 15) or even "comical" (25).

Regarding a woman like Paulina, who has "no mind or life of her own, but must necessarily live, move, and have her being in another", as "cursed", Lucy "often wished she [Paulina] would mind herself" (V 25). According to Piehler, "this overall introduction of the narrative and the narrator appears to link space, particularly interiors, with identity. Both the reader's recognition of Lucy Snow and her own self-realization develop from spatial description and dynamics" (V 45). This reveals that Lucy cannot restrain her internal feelings while attempting to be an objective observer. Lucy's remarks represent the difference between her and Paulina's backgrounds, and Lucy implies that her life before coming to Bretton was very harsh. After spending a peaceful six months in

Bretton, she returns to the house of kinsfolk who had taken her over initially, and the narrator mentions that "I too well remember a time—a long time, of cold, of danger of contention" (*V* 35). This means that Lucy, like Jane Eyre, may have been abused by her relatives and disciplined to be quiet and reserved as a liminal woman. Her repetition of the phrase "I [had] no home" (*V* 50) demonstrates that she does not know her family, home, or domestic happiness; even the Brettons and their house are not identified by Lucy as her family or home. Fourteen-year-old Lucy is cognisant that both she and Paulina will have to endure the oppression of being liminal women. She expresses sympathy with the displaced child by embracing Paulina, who is trembling in her bed, and wonders: "How will she get through this world, or battle this life?" (*V* 57); despite Lucy's anxiety, ten years later, the seventeen-year-old Paulina appears before her as the daughter of the Count de Bassompierre with grace and maiden innocence in the drawing room of Mrs Bretton in Villette. Thus, the episode in Bretton highlights Lucy's rootless social identity in contrast to the Brettons and the Homes. However, unlike Paulina, Lucy does not try to adjust herself to the middle-class household by performing the role of a proper lady; rather, she prefers being outside the bounds of a middle-class existence and blames Paulina for depending too heavily on her male guardians.

Lucy first finds employment as a caregiver for Miss Marchmont, an elderly sick lady with rheumatism residing in a handsome residence. Mary Jacobus mentions, "[a]s a middle-class woman, Lucy can only be employed within the home ... but that 'home', since she is employee not 'mistress', must remain alien" (46–47). However, Lucy's future as an unmarried and abandoned woman is foreshadowed through this experience serving her employer. She describes:

> Two hot, close rooms [Miss Marchmont's drawing-room and bedroom] thus became my world; and a crippled old woman, my mistress, my friend, my all. Her service was my duty—her pain, my suffering—her relief, my hope—her anger, my punishment—her regard, my reward. I forgot that there were fields, woods, rivers, seas, an ever-changing sky outside the steam-dimmed lattice of this sick chamber; I was almost content to forget it. All within me became narrowed to my lot. (*V* 37)

Becoming used to looking after her all day long, Lucy also forgets the outside world and does not hope to get out of the confined space, which highlights the limited and often debilitating life choices available to an orphaned, penniless woman. Miss Marchmont's situation reveals the circumstances of single women in the Victorian Age, who were provided only a small, restricted space. According to Diane Long Hoeveler, Miss Marchmont is "Lucy's first double" and is "wounded by abandonment and has escaped into a disengaged stance toward life" (226); Miss Marchmont has lived as a recluse following her lover's death, which mirrors Lucy's situation at the end of the novel where her lover also dies while returning to her. Thus, Lucy Snowe, in the opening chapters, rarely talks about herself because she does not have to; she finds a part of herself in the women she meets. However, unlike the women she meets, Lucy gains her own voice and place through her mobility and journey.

According to Anthony Giddens, "modernity is a post-traditional order", and "the question, 'How shall I live?' has to be answered in day-to-day decisions about how to behave, what to wear and what to eat—and many other things—as well as interpreted within the temporal unfolding of self-identity" (14). These questions and the answers often lead to self-discovery. Lucy's experience of performing on stage at the school requires her to decide how to behave and what to wear metaphorically; this leads her to a transformative experience. As Piehler argues, "while Lucy may not obviously be a volcanic presence like Vashti, this moment that includes her preparation and performance transforms her into a creative figure for her theatrical audience and herself" (65). Although Lucy is cautious not to be conspicuous in a gown of "purple-gray" (*V* 131), the colour of "dun mist", on the day of Madame Beck's fete, she is asked suddenly to act the part of a man who is talkative and fluffy in a school play by M. Paul—the professor of literature. Lucy is led to "the solitary and lofty attic" by him, "put in and locked in" (*V* 135) the place, and he takes the key with him and vanished. Of course, he does not intend to confine her in the attic like "Bluebeard" (*V* 137); however, he thinks that she should be left there alone to learn her lines within the few hours left before the play begins. She describes the attic as an unpleasant place, as it is "hot as Africa" in summer and "cold as Greenland" (*V* 135) in winter. The attic is cluttered with boxes and lumber and has cobwebs in the ceiling and creatures, such as rats, black beetles, and cockroaches. Lucy realises that it is the darkness of the attic that birthed the rumour that the ghost of a nun had once been seen there. While she is shocked by the unpleasantness of the attic at first, her discovery and opening of the skylight lets in the fresh air and allows her to renovate her surroundings:

> Underneath this aperture I pushed a large empty chest, and having mounted upon it a smaller box, and wiped from both the dust, I gathered my dress...fastidiously around me, ascended this species

of extempore throne, and being seated, commenced the acquisition of my task. (*V* 135)

Her wiping the dust from a large chest and a small box to create a makeshift seat mirrors her cleaning of the rustic seat in the allée défendue (the narrow path) in the school garden later in the narrative. As Zuzanna Jakubowski points out, "Lucy draws an explicit connection between the garden sanctuary and the attic" (101). Indeed, the attic's remoteness from any other room and its gloom described as "partial darkness obscured one end" (*V* 135), which leads to the rumour of the nun's ghost, are similar to the "seclusion" and "gloom" (108) of the allée défendue. Similar to how Lucy had a sense of closeness to the quiet and shady narrow path, she comes to regard the small box as a royal "throne" (*V* 135)—her comfortable seat. According to Piehler, "the attic's qualities" like "architectural height" and "a remoteness from the physical world" connotes "a closeness to the activities of the mind and the creative imagination" (65). Indeed, Lucy concentrates on learning her lines in the solitary and lofty attic, going so far as to change the character of her role to suit her. When finally, M. Paul calls for Lucy, she describes the experience of leaving the attic with resentment:

> In a moment my throne was abdicated, the attic evacuated; an inverse repetition of the impetus which had brought me up into the attic, instantly took me down—down—down to the very kitchen. I thought I should have gone to the cellar. (*V* 137)

According to Piehler, "along with speeding through the levels of the building, Lucy has spontaneously decided to act, to open herself to an audience" (*V* 66) on the stage. The rapid speed of the movement from the private space of the attic to the public space downstairs thrusts her into modernity. According to Susan Stanford Friedman, "the velocity, acceleration, and dynamism of shattering change across a wide spectrum of societal institutions are key components of modernity" (433). Indeed, the speed of mobility is valued in modernity. However, upon being ushered into the small cabinet that acted as the green room, Lucy is "dazzled", "deafened" and "stifled" and feels the room "choking" her (*V* 138). In the chaotic greenroom, Lucy decidedly refuses a man's costume as it "would not suit me [her]" (*V* 138). She insists that she should dress herself in her own way and retains her woman's garb by adding a man's vest, collar, cravat and coat and making up her back hair close with a man's hat in her hand. Thus, wearing both women's and men's clothes simultaneously, she destroys the gender code of dressing. According to Jakubowski, "Lucy ... displays herself as a being of transgression passing 'in-betweenness'" (102). I think that Lucy's costume exists within the domain of in-betweenness and creates her own unique appearance. Similar to how the greenroom is situated "between" "the first classe" and "the grand salle" (*V* 138), the allée défendue is situated "between" the girls' school and boys' school. Lucy, in-betweenness, insists that the costume in-betweenness is suitable for her role. According to Judith Butler, constructing a specific identity that distinguishes between the male and female is impossible:

> The construction of coherent sexual identity along the disjunctive axis of the feminine/masculine is bound to fail; the disruptions of this coherence through the inadvertent reemergence of the repressed reveal not only that 'identity' is constructed, but that the prohibition

that constructs identity is inefficacious. (39)

Thus, forcing the clothing code on the basis of gender ignores the construction of identity. Although Lucy's costume seems transgressive initially, M. Paul permits her to wear the contrived costume, and the audience and Dr John understand and admire her performance. According to Tony Tanner, "Lucy's own ambiguous...relish in her man's role in the play is certainly a symptom of repressed or slightly distorted elements in her character" (35). I think that her hidden mannish energy and nature bursts out during her stage performance. For example, it is not the crowd but her "own voice" (*V* 140) that frightens her on the bright stage. However, helped by M. Paul's advice to "imagine yourself in the garret, acting to the rat" (*V* 206), she restores her normal voice and thinks only about the parsonage she represents:

> By-and-by, feeling the right power come—the spring demanded gush and rise inwardly—I became sufficiently composed to notice my fellow actors.... I recklessly altered the spirit of the role. Without heart, without interest, I could not play it at all. It must be played—in went the yearned-for seasoning—thus favoured, I played it with relish. (*V* 140)

Her movement from the gloomy attic, a segregated and private space, to the bright stage, a public space, awakens her previously unperceived creative powers. Lucy discovers her own inherent faculty and voice, which she wants to represent through the play. She reflects on how her role and the play should be performed and decides to act to "please myself" (*V* 141), not to satisfy others. While preparing for her part, she modifies the given part to create a more favourable role for her; however, the next day, she admits that "to cherish and exercise this newfound faculty might gift me with a world of delight, but it would not do for a mere looker-on at life" (*V* 141). While she is aware of her inherent "strength" and "longing" (*V* 141), she dares to avoid the "delight" world where she exposes them and retreats to the shady space. According to Zuzanna Jakubowski, "through her transgression and appropriation of spatial contrasts she tears down dichotomic oppositions and defines these spaces—and through them herself—as 'in-between' and therefore resisting a society that categorizes according to binary oppositions of age, class, race, and gender" (102). Indeed, identifying herself as "in-between", Lucy challenges and transgresses the dichotomy of gender, class, and nationality. However, she does not exist within the marginality but is in the process of giving rise to "a something different, something new, and unrecognizable" (Bhabha 211). According to Linda McDowell, "the 'in-between' is itself a process or a dynamic, not just a stage on the way to a more final identity" (215). Lucy has a mobile nature and reflects on her past and future actions. In the scene of the Lottery following the concert, Lucy wins a cigar case, while Dr John gains a lady's headdress, and despite his request to exchange their winnings, she refuses. Her subsequent possession of the cigar case illustrates her mannish character. According to Anthony Giddens, self-identity is "the self as reflexively understood by the person in terms of her or his biography" (53). As Giddens points out, "a person's identity is not to be found in behaviour" but "in the capacity to keep a particular narrative going" (54). Consequently, writing her own life's narrative allows Lucy to perceive her identity and conceal her inherently strong nature by deliberately disguising herself as a looker-on throughout the novel.

There are two sites where Lucy has the opportunities to contemplate and rebel against the identity imposed on women by Victorian society. Visiting the art museum and the theatre, even if Lucy is taken there by Dr John, provides her with the contemplative space to become aware of her consciousness and begin her opposition as a woman who is compelled to the limits. Liana F. Piehler calls these places "framed spaces" by borrowing Tony Tanner's term and argues that they seem "necessary for solidifying a certain sureness of identity and expression in Lucy through narrative" (60). Lucy's impression, perception and imagination are strengthened and shift from the domain of the accepted into that of the affirmative and transgressive within these spaces with boundaries from the surroundings, where some themes are concentrated. According to Michel Foucault, both the museum and the theatre are heterotopic spaces. Foucault defines heterotopias as a real place in contrast to the utopia, the unreal place:

> There are also, probably in every culture, in every civilization, real places—places that do exist and that are formed in the very founding of society—which are something like counter-sites, a kind of effectively enacted utopia in which the real sites, all the other real sites that can be found within the culture, are simultaneously represented, contested, and inverted. Places of this kind are outside of all places, even though it may be possible to indicate their location in reality. (1998; 231)

Using this enigmatic definition of heterotopic spaces, Jakubowski claims that "it is the museum and the theatre where Lucy and the reader find feminine identity 'represented,' 'contested', and 'inverted'" (103). Lucy states that she enjoys visiting art museums, especially being left there alone until Dr John calls for her after his work. Her observation of the paintings is intended for "examining, questioning, and forming conclusions" regarding them (*V* 198). While it is unclear whether her critical eye for paintings is dependable, the painting titled "Cleopatra" is unpleasant to her. This picture of portentous size is displayed with consideration, and a cushioned bench is set in front of it. The woman in the picture is "larger than the life" and seems to be "the queen of the collection" (*V* 199) at the museum:

> She was, indeed, extremely well fed: very much butcher's meat—to say nothing of bread, vegetables, and liquids—must she have consumed to attain that breadth and height, that wealth of muscle, that affluence of flesh. She lay half-reclined on a coach... she ought to have been standing, or at least sitting bolt upright. She had no business to lounge away the noon on a sofa. She ought likewise to have worn decent garments... she managed to make inefficient raiment. (*V* 199–200)

Lucy's commentary is far from a criticism of the work of art. She harshly criticises the woman's "wealth of muscle", "affluence of fresh", her being depicted as reclining on a couch, having "no business" and not wearing clothes. Lucy's criticism focuses on Cleopatra's plump, amorous figure and slovenliness. Or rather, Lucy might recognise the history of Egypt, the political tactics and extravagance of the queen known as a woman of great beauty; therefore, she cannot admit the queen as a woman who seduced Caesar and Antony with her beauty to retain the Ptolemaic Dynasty. According to Michel Foucault, in the museum, "there are heterotopias of accumulating time...the will to enclose in one place all times, all epochs, all forms, all tastes...in an immobile place...belongs to our modernity" (1998; 242). While Lucy perceives that the picture of Cleopatra was imagined and painted by an artist in the Renaissance or later and has been selected to be displayed as a valuable work in the museum, she opposes the concept of women's beauty or female identity, which a male-dominated society has assigned. When she comes across M. Paul in the museum, Lucy listens to his conception of female identity. He animadverts on seeing her alone in the museum looking at the sensuous portrait of Cleopatra. He considers that Lucy, a young woman, should be accompanied by Dr Bretton's mother and only look at the four pictures worthy of appreciation; he proceeds to show her a set of four pictures entitled "La vie d'une femme" (the life of a woman):

> They were painted rather in a remarkable style—flat, dead, pale, and formal. The first represented a "Jeune Fille" (young woman), coming out of a church-door, a missal in her hand...the image of a most villainous little precocious she-hypocrite. The second, a "Mariée" (wife), with a long white veil, kneeling at a prie-dieu in her chamber.... The third, a "Jeune Mere" (young mother) hanging disconsolate over a clayey and puffy baby.... The fourth, a "Veuve" (widow) being a black woman, holding by the hand a black little girl, and the twain studiously surveying an elegant French monument. (*V* 201–02)

Lucy regards these four women as "grim and grey as burglars" and "cold and vapid as ghosts" (*V* 202). While the notion that women must endure hard, miserable, and passive lives was quite common in the Victorian age, Lucy absolutely rejects it and is contemptuous of these weak women. As Foucault points out that the museum "enclose all times,… all tastes in one place" (1998; 242), the opposite features of women like "Cleopatra" and "La vie d'une femme" allow Lucy to affirm that she will never become either of them. As Piehler argues, "what she [Lucy] most valued was her solitude and own 'space' for viewing the paintings, the privacy and room to view the images, contemplate them, and assess them for herself" (62). Consequently, spaces such as the art museum force her to consider how a woman should live her life and contributes to her finding her own identity by transgressing the norms of society.

Lucy is also affected by the impression left by a famous actress who acts as a royal Vashti in the theatre, the heterotopic space. The actress appears on the stage and responds to Lucy's long-cherished anticipations:

> She rose at nine that December night: above the horizon I saw her come. She could shine yet with pale grandeur and steady might; but that star verged already on its judgement-day. Seen near, it was a chaos—hollow, half-consumed: an orb perished or perishing—half lava, half glow. (*V* 257)

Although Lucy is seated quite close to the stage and can view the proceedings from up close, the actress is described as an abstract being, "a chaos", "hollow", and "an orb". According to Piehler, these expressions reveal "Vashti's identity—a violent, ever transforming entity, revolting yet powerfully attractive" (63). Lucy perceives that the actress of Vashti is "her something neither of woman nor of man" (*V* 257) with evil forces in her eyes, and that the play is "a spectacle low, horrible, immoral"

(258). As Foucault points out, "the theatre brings onto the rectangle of the stage, one after the other, a whole series of places that are foreign to one another" (1998; 241). Lucy watches Vashti's "struggle" and "resistance" in the places of "revel" and "war" and realises that even though she is "fallen, insurgent, and banished", Vashti's exile is illuminated by "Heaven's light" (*V* 258). Thus, as Foucault argues, on "the rectangle of the stage" (1998; 241), the marvellous spectacles are performed one after the other, thereby creating a space "outside of all places" (1998; 239). In contrast to the admiration she feels for the struggling Vashti throughout the tragedy, Lucy rebukes the artist of Cleopatra. She insists that he should "come and sit down and study this different vision" of Vashti. "The mighty muscle", "the abounding blood" and "the full-fed flesh" (*V* 258), which he worshipped are, in her opinion, only illusions of "the materialists" (*V* 258). Lucy writes that "scarcely a substance herself, she [Vashti] grapples to conflict with abstractions" (*V* 258). As Jakubowski argues, "Lucy seems to identify herself with Vashti's struggle" (105). In addition, I think that the displaced Lucy's sympathy for the exiled Vashti connotes modernity. According to Rita Felski, modernity "celebrates mobility, movement, exile, boundary crossing" (5). Recognising that Vashti is "wicked", Lucy emphasises and admires Vashti's "strength" (*V* 258) to try to rebel against and destroy the abstract oppression by society. As Lucy challenges to cross the gendered boundaries set by society, she seems to experience modernity. Finding that Dr John does not sympathise with the "wild" and "intense" (*V* 259) performance of the actress, Lucy considers that he regards the actress "as a woman, not an artist" (260). This demonstrates that Lucy has the capacity to appreciate and assimilate the transgressed artistic space in modernity, which is "outside of all the places", as Foucault suggests, unlike other people in the Victorian age. Thus, in the heterotopic space, Lucy recognises her transgressed nature and her potential faculty to accept modernity.

At the festival in Villette, while listening to a grand concert among the crowd, Lucy is offered a chair by a bookseller who has a business relationship with the Rue Fossette. However, his kindness brings her near the "familiar and domestic group" (*V* 456) of the Brettons and the de Bassompierres. Lucy is uneasy at being seated so close to them as she likes to mingle with "the silent, unknown, consequently unaccosted neighbour" of "citizens" and "plebeians", and she is eager to be only "the distant gazer at" the middle-class people with "the silk robe, the velvet mantle, and the plumed chapeau" (*V* 455). Lucy wants to keep a distance from the bourgeois like Mrs Bretton and Miss de Bassompierre because "it suited me to be alone" among "so much life and joy" (*V* 455). However, only Dr John Bretton is aware of the existence of Lucy behind him. When he rises and contrives to approach her, Lucy "implied, by sort of supplicatory gesture, that it was my prayer to be let alone" (*V* 457). Looking at her, he finally gives up his attempts to approach or call her. Although Lucy denies Dr John's indifference to her, she admits his misunderstanding of her nature; he thinks that she is "quite tame, or absolutely inoffensive and shadowlike":

> [B]y long and equal kindness, he proved to me that he kept one little closet, over the door of which was written "Lucy's Room". I kept a place for him, too—a place of which I never took the measure, either by rule or compass: I think it was like the tent of Peri-Banou. All my life long I carried it folded in the hollow of my hand yet, released from that hold and constriction, I know not but it innate capacity for expanse might have magnified it into a tabernacle for a host. (*V* 457)

Although Lucy admires Dr John's philanthropy and his friendship, she notices that he relishes in the popularity that his philanthropy brings him among the wretched and is offended by his insensitivity in asking Lucy to accompany him when obtaining permission to marry Paulina from M. de Bassompierre. Lucy affirms that Dr John prepares "a little closet" for her in his "goodly mansion" (*V* 457), which is created by his imagination in his head; the closet is a bourgeois domestic ideal place, which has a segregated wall, and it can be used similar to how he shut the child Polly out of the dining room. In contrast, she carries "the tent" (*V* 457) for him, which can be freely folded, and whose length and width she has not measured by rule or compass. According to Jakubowski, "Lucy forgoes any social measures ("rule or compass") and professes her inner self freed from the prison ("hold and restriction") of a domesticated consciousness" (106). Indeed, Lucy transgresses or tries to destroy the gendered boundaries and the force imposed by the authorities and seeks freedom. The instance of Lucy carrying the folded tent in her hand portrays a nomadic image and her mobile nature. According to Tim Cresswell, "the lived experience of exiles, migrants, and refugees is tied to the need to think nomadically. Mobile lives need nomad thought to make a new kind of thought" (44). Lucy, a migrant to a foreign country and a seeker of refuge, always embraces the nomadic image of a mobile person. "[T]abernacle" (*V* 457) also has the religious resonance of the portable sanctuary. According to Sandra M. Gilbert and Susan Gubar, by holding the folded tent that can expand into a tabernacle for him in the hollow of her hand, Lucy "admits for the first time her love for Dr John", and she "nevertheless avoids making herself known" (435). I disagree with this argument, as Lucy buries her love for him along with his letters in the school garden prior to this scene upon discovering the relationship between Dr John and Paulina. Since she can throw away the portable tent at her discretion, Lucy is in a more favourable position than Dr John Graham. As Tony Tanner argues, "Graham's will to impose roles is connected to the subtly tyranny of the male in this world" (17). Lucy says, "I realize his entire misapprehension of my character and nature. He always wanted to give me a role not mine. Nature and I opposed him" (*V* 318). Thus, she has internally opposed him for a long time despite cherishing feelings for him.

When Lucy is saved by Dr John outside the Catholic Church and brought to the small cabinet with sea-green walls in his house, she describes it as if it had been in the sea:

> My calm little room seemed somehow like a cave in the sea. There was no colour about it, except that white and pale green, suggestive of foam and deep water; the blanched cornice was adorned with shell-shaped ornaments, and there were white mouldings like dolphins... the red satin pincushion bore affinity to coral; even that dark, shining glass might have mirrored a mermaid... a world so high above that the rush of its largest waves, the dash of its fiercest breakers, could sound down in this submarine home, only like murmurs and a lullaby. (*V* 181)

As Dr John Bretton's house, built in the old style of the Basse-Ville, is situated on the high ground, the gale against the house-front of the little room sounds like "a tide retiring from a shore" (*V* 181). Lucy, whose body is weakened, lies on the bed and falls into a dreamlike state, where she feels as if she were "a mermaid" in "the cave in the sea" (*V* 181). According to Liana F. Piehler, "Lucy's spectral mirror image is replaced with the possibility of a mermaid, a creature of feminine mystery and allure" (58). Knowing that Dr John Bretton, who is fascinated by Ginevra, does not have any romantic interests in her, Lucy is afraid that she will fall in love with him and be tormented physically and mentally. Thus, Dr John's little room is not "a very safe asylum" (V 171) for Lucy, and its smallness makes it feel "confining" to her (172). According to Tony Tanner, "it [the little room] is not a home but an 'asylum' where she [Lucy] can convalesce but not pursue a life in society such as she must do if she is to establish an identity rather than secure a hiding place for her ailing self" (13). It is the home where she can establish the identity that she seeks for herself. Lucy realises that the womanly figure, who is like a mermaid, in the little room, which is like a cave in the sea, is not her true self. She acknowledges the difference between Mrs Bretton's life and hers. Comparing Mrs Bretton's life to the ship, Lucy describes it as "the stately ship cruising safe on smooth seas, with its full complement of crew, a captain gay and brave, and venturous and provident" (V 181). On the other hand, Lucy's is "the life-boat" that always "lie[s] dry and solitary in an old, dark boat-house, only putting to sea when the billows run high in rough weather, when cloud encounters water, when danger and death divide between them the rule of the great deep" (V 181). The Brettons' ship does not run any risks and always navigates the calm sea, while Lucy's boat floats on the rough sea and braves danger to head toward unknown destinations. Michel Foucault argues that "the ship is a heterotopia par excellence" (1998; 244). Foucault says about the boat:

> [T]he boat is a floating piece of space, a place without a place, that exists by itself, that is closed in on itself and at the same time is given over to the infinity of the sea and that , from port to port, from tack

to tack, ... it goes as far as the colonies in search of the most precious treasures they conceal in their gardens, you will understand why the boat has not only been for our civilization, from the sixteenth century until the present, the great instrument of economic development..., but has been simultaneously the greatest reserve of the imagination. (1998; 244)

Foucault's boat strangely corresponds to Lucy's boat rather than Mrs Bretton's. Lucy's metaphorical boat is also "a floating piece of space, a place without a place", which is aimed at the unknown but boundless space—"the infinity of the sea" (Foucault 1998; 244), and serves as the instrument of her economic development and independence in modernity, with Lucy's fertile imagination. In contrast to Lucy's boat, Mrs Bretton's ship remains in the safe space, which is "not a modern place" (*V* 182), "this country site", "about half a league without the Porte de Crey" (177). Thus, Lucy acknowledges that the metaphorical boat of her life faces challenging situations and navigates the modernising world for her economic development, freedom and independence.

On the balcony surrounded by the gardens of the faubourg, Lucy shows domestic hospitality as a hostess for the first time toward M. Paul. Acquiring her own house and career and seeing the prospect of her independence and marriage to M Paul, Lucy begins to speak in her own voice: "I spoke. All escaped from my lips. I lacked not words now; fast I narrated; fluent I told my tale; it streamed on my tongue" (*V* 490). While she used to fear her own voice and confine it in others' domestic or public spaces both in England and Villette, she now liberates her voice and represents her true self in her new house. As Tanner argues, "speaking in her own way within the book is related to narrating the book itself in her own way" (42). During that time, M. Paul gives up "his own system of repression" (*V* 491), listens to her story, and even spurs her to speak with his smile. His attitude is transformed from that of patriarchal oppression into a generous and considerate one. The relationship between Lucy and M. Paul seems to be one founded on mutual understanding and trust. She is no longer inoffensive, shadowlike, looker-on at the world, and solitary; instead, she places herself in her space as a heroine in her story. Having amassed confidence, she no longer cares how others see her. According to Gilbert and Gubar, Lucy has to "seek her identity on foreign soil because she is metaphorically a foreigner even in England" (405). Indeed, Lucy, a displaced orphan, leaves her country and discovers herself as an individual rather than as an Englishwoman in a foreign country. As Diane Long Hoeveler argues:

> [Lucy] is led by M. Paul—her masculinized inner faculty—to a proper assessment of herself and her place in the world.... In the process of writing her story, Lucy relives her mistaken perceptions and, as a type of artist, exorcises the past in a new and created vision. (239)

Indeed, now that she admits her inner masculine strength, she does not have to conceal her true self within in-betweenness as she writes her story. According to Anthony Giddens, "the essential question of self-identity is bound up with the fragile nature of the biography which the individual 'supplies' about herself. A person's identity is...in the capacity to keep a particular narrative going" (54). Lucy's identity is revealed as the narrative unfolds; however, the open ending confuses us. "That storm roared frenzied, for seven days. It did not cease till the Atlantic was strewn with wrecks: it did not lull till the deeps had gorged their full of sustenance" (*V* 495). While Lucy tries to avoid the information regarding M. Paul's shipwreck, it is clear that he does not return to Villette from the southwest colony. While his mobility is brought to an end by the dangers of modernity, Lucy spends this period as "the three happiest years" (*V* 493) of her life. Having acquired the inheritance from Miss Marchmont, she rents the house adjoining hers and opens a pensionnat (boarding school) for girls. However, this ending is to be anticipated, even though Brontë's father opposed M. Paul's death. Although M. Paul provided Lucy with "a legacy" (*V* 494), such as "a thought for present" and " a motive" for the future, he had to be punished by "abandon(ing) justice" and "serv(ing) the ends of selfishness" (495) in the West Indian isle by order of Rome and the group of Madame Walravens; furthermore, his death liberates Lucy from the duty of "the steward of his property" (*V* 493) and the oppression of patriarchal authority. The fact that Lucy, who compares herself to a "life-boat", does not rescue the drowning Paul reveals that she no more needs an adviser and a husband. Gaining her voice, Lucy produces her identity through teaching at her own school and writing her story and by cherishing the memory of M. Paul between the house he chose and the pensionnat she built. She voyaged across the sea, migrated to a foreign country, and established her own girls' school with no class-based boundaries; "pupils came—burghers at first—a higher class ere long" (*V* 493). Her migration makes her realise and produce an identity of in-betweenness, which is independent of the patriarchal repression in the faubourg(suburb) of Villette, the international city. According to Tim Cresswell, "identities are produced and performed through mobility" (44). Lucy's mobility realises her production of identity and makes her transgress the boundaries of countries, class, and gender, and encourages her to go forward as an immigrant in the modernising society. As Rita Felski argues, modernity "celebrates mobility, movements, exile, and boundary crossing" (23), and thus, Brontë creates a protagonist who appreciates modernity and challenges the norms of the Victorian era.

3.3. *North and South*

While Margaret Hale in *North and South* is not an orphan like Jane Eyre in *Jane Eyre* or Lucy Snowe in *Villette*, her displacement is nevertheless represented at the beginning of the novel. Margaret has been left at her wealthy aunt Shaw's house in London for ten years to obtain appropriate education and accomplishments to become a middle-class lady. She is only allowed to visit Helstone—her home where her parents live—during "her bright holidays" (*NS* 7). The child Margaret somewhat recognises that the economic circumstances of Mr Hale, the clergyman of Helstone church, prevent him from being able to afford a nursery or a governess. Although Margaret is reared with care by Mrs Shaw as if she were a daughter, the labour she is expected to undertake to assist Mrs Shaw and Edith brings her closer to the servant's position. In addition to writing letters and making a list for a party in place of Edith, her aid in organising Edith's wedding leaves her very exhausted and "oppressed" (*NS* 13) with weariness. At the house in Harley Street, she acknowledges that she has to play "the part of Figaro" (*NS* 17), the character in Rossini's opera who is used by everyone, and opines that she has to be "docile to her aunt's laws" (406) as a lodger and she is sensitive to Mrs Shaw's facial expression. According to Divya Athmanathan, Mrs Shaw's house on Harley Street represents "the hybridity of Margaret's personality" and attributes "a dual class status to her" (39). Indeed, while Margaret has a repulsive feeling about Mrs Shaw's interference in dictating that a footman should accompany Edith and Margaret, she obeys her aunt unquestioningly. Similarly, she rides the coach quietly even when she wants to walk to follow her aunt's dictum.

Additionally, Margaret has to get Edith's Indian shawls from the attic instead of Edith, who is napping on the sofa in the back drawing room, when Mrs Shaw wants to show them to her guests. Furthermore, Margaret obeys her aunt passively and takes on the role of shawl-bearer in front of the mirror in the drawing room: "as she was turned round, she caught a glimpse of herself in the mirror... and smiled at her own appearance there—the familiar features in the usual garb of a princess" (*NS* 11). She recognises that, when wearing Edith's gorgeous shawls, her reflection in the mirror looks akin to that of a princess and that she enjoys being "dressed in such splendour" (*NS* 11). Thus, she embraces her feminine sensibility to see her own appearance in the mirror; however, she expects Henry Lennox to sympathise with her sense of "ludicrousness" (*NS* 11). According to Michel Foucault:

> [T]he mirror makes [the] place that I occupy at the moment when I look at myself in the glass at once absolutely real, connected with all the space that surrounds it, and absolutely unreal, since in order to be perceived it has to pass through this virtual point which is over there"; in this respect, the mirror functions as "a heterotopia". (1998; 240)

Considering Foucault's concept of a heterotopic space, Margaret's recognition upon awakening from her femininity reflected in the unreal space of the mirror reaffirms that she is far from femininity in the real space and thinks light of it. Here, it should be remarked that while Margaret usually hates the coach as the symbol of materialism, she longs for the luxurious Indian shawls, which are associated with materialism, modernity and imperialism. Such a hybrid nature of Margaret misleads Henry Lennox and leads to him misunderstanding her personality. Henry considers her a traditionally feminine woman and proposes marriage; however, she rejects him because she knows that he is contemptuous of women. In reality, Margaret is more practical and active than the empty-headed and dependent Edith and often writes letters or makes invitations for dinner in Edith's place. Margaret is excited to hear about the picturesque and adventurous life in Corfu from Captain Lennox, Edith's fiancé, while Edith is frightened by her future life abroad as she prefers a good house in a rich district in London to an unknown life in a foreign country. As Patricia Ingham points out, "Margaret Hale does not remain a standard middle-class stereotype/heroine and that the narrator's perspective on this changing self is not conventionally 'feminine'" (56). Returning to her home—Helstone—after Edith's marriage, Margaret realises her dream of "filling the important post of only daughter in Helstone parsonage" (*NS* 8) and enjoys walking in the forest freely. Her adaptability to life with people in the forest is revealed in her language: she at once learned and felt delighted in using their peculiar words. "[L]anguage is tied to identity" (Scholl 101), and Margaret, by speaking the same way as the inhabitants in the forest, succeeds in having a good relationship with them. Indeed, after nine years of absence from her home, eighteen-year-old Margaret adapts herself to her home as an inhabitant for the first time and starts seeing Helstone as a practical place. Thus, when she is asked by Lennox what Helstone was like in Harley Street, she answers embarrassedly that "all the other places in

England that I have seen seem so hard and prosaic-looking…. Helstone is like a village in a poem—in one of Tennyson's poems" (*NS* 14). Thus, while she holds a deep nostalgia for Helstone, she could not depict it concretely and instead escapes to literary images during her long stay on Harley Street. The meaning of home for Margaret is created through comparison with the experiences of "other places" like London, which seems relatively hard and "prosaic-looking". According to Wendy Parkins, "very early in the novel, then, an idea of home is invoked—as an assured sense of place in the modern world—which the forthcoming dramatic changes will demonstrate is a precarious notion indeed" (2009; 25). Indeed, Margaret loves her home, Helstone, because it is neither ordinary nor boring but full of various changes. As Parkins points out, Margaret "does not fit the conventional representation of the domestic bourgeois woman", and she is linked to "a disorder associated with change and upheaval—a response more typical of the modern masculine subject" (2009; 25). Misunderstanding her nature, Henry Lennox conceives that her love for her home stems from her traditional personality. However, her characterisation of gardening as "such hard work" (*NS* 14), reveals that she is not always a country girl but a woman with sophisticated taste gained in the upper-middle-class society in London. Thus, Margaret shows her hybrid nature whereby she loves country life in Helstone while simultaneously hating gardening, which was considered "a proper employment for young ladies in the country" (*NS* 14).

Margaret's faculty to make arrangements for their shift to Milton contrasts Mr Hale's incompetence. Her practical management of their shift to the northern industrial town leads her to usurp the patriarchal decision-making role of Mr Hale, who has been too much of a coward to inform his wife of their expulsion from Helstone and asks Margaret to do so. Margaret sympathises with her invalid mother, who suffers from the bad news of their move, and shows a maidenly sensibility to comfort her. However, despite her own sadness, she has "a touch of the old gentleman about her" (*NS* 49), as Dixon, Mrs Hale's maid, observes. Margaret has both a womanly kindness to snuggle close to her depressed mother and a mannish "determined" (*NS* 49) manner. She becomes irritated with her parents for not preparing for their journey and implores her father to do so. Shifting her emotional gears, Margaret prepares for their move, which reveals her practical nature. Here, it is notable that Margaret is obedient to her father and does not complain of his obscure and selfish explanation for leaving the Church and Helstone, which he had not discussed even with his wife despite it being such an important matter. Thus, it is said that Margaret is initially docile to patriarchy in the Victorian age, but after their shift to Milton, she begins to take over his patriarchal decisions. Margaret's identity tied to the post of the daughter in the Helstone parsonage is eliminated when her father decides to leave the Church. Simultaneously, she loses her identity tied to her beloved home—Helstone—and becomes dislocated again. While Margaret loses her identity as a daughter of the Helstone parsonage upon their arrival at Milton, she is still proud of belonging to the middle class. Thornton is surprised at young Margaret's "straight, fearless, dignified" figure, "a different type to most of those he was in the habit of seeing" (*NS* 62) at first sight. Her beauty demonstrates that she is confident in herself as a middle-class lady who acquires decency and education despite being the daughter of a mere clergyman.

According to Patricia Ingham, "Margaret's specifically middle-class beauty is apparently that of the Angel", and Thornton regards it as "indicative of perfect womanly" (*NS* 58). Indeed, the woman who shows the sophisticated manner in the drawing room is an ideal angel; however, Margaret's "short curled upper lip, the round, massive upturned chin, the manner of carrying her head, her movements, full of a soft feminine defiance" gives Thornton the impression of "haughtiness" (*NS* 63). Thus, her appearance creates one of two impressions on the people she meets in Milton: Thornton has the impression of not only her beauty but also her haughtiness, which he attributes to her middle-class upbringing, while Higgins admires her attractiveness by calling her "your bonny face". The narrator describes that "her mouth was wide; no rosebud that could only open just enough to let out a 'yes' and 'no'" (*NS* 18). As Patsy Stoneman points out, Margaret's wide mouth represents her "straight-speaking" (84) attitude to clearly insist on her own opinion, unlike Lucy in *Villette*. According to Lesa Scholl, "it is not just Margaret's physical mobility, but her willingness to be mobile in her use of language that enables her to communicate effectively across cultures, as well as to mediate between them" (96). Indeed, Margaret's use of language effectively creates her identity as not only a mediator between the cultures of the north and south but also a communicator between them.

Thus, we can see the hybridity in Margaret's personality. Linda McDowell, a geographer, explains:

> Hybridity, as used by cultural theorists such as Stuart Hall, merely means that identities and cultural forms are a product of intermingling and fusion, a product of movement. The term has, however, been used in a range of somewhat different ways. It has been used in association with images that suggest an identity between two

competing worlds: to refer to those who seem to live on the borders or in the margins. (212)

In Milton, Margaret's position becomes ambiguous within the margins of the industrial city, where she is no longer the daughter of a clergyman, but the daughter of a tutor of classics for factory owners like Thornton, whose ostentatious mother looks down on Mr Hale as a poor tutor. However, Margaret's social displacement from a middle-class position makes it easy for her to associate with working-class people, such as Higgins and Bessy. Visiting their house as a friend, not as the daughter of a clergyman, makes it possible for her to build an intimacy with them. According to Patricia Ingham, "Margaret's own sense of identity is fractured" because "she is middle-class, in her own terms, in tastes, feeling and values but with no social group that shares them. Her sense of her class as a constituent of identity is destabilised" (61). Indeed, Margaret's heated argument with Thornton, who believes in capitalist modernity and the development of machinery, calls his workers "hands" and ignores their demands, stems from not only her sense of justice but from her sympathy with working-class people like the Higginses. As Ingham points out, Margaret is an "outcast" (61) vis-à-vis the middle class and her home in the south, like the Higginses, who are outcasts from their home, Burnley-ways, which is forty miles to the north of Milton. Higgins' reference to their relationship: "*North and South* has both met and made kind of friends in this big smoky place" (*NS* 73), has a symbolic connotation that both outcasts serve as agents linking the different standpoints.

Margaret defends herself using "factory slang" (*NS* 233) when her mother, who was a ward of Sir John Beresford, reproves her. According to Athmanathan, "at this moment, the spatial context of an industrial town structures her [Margaret's] identity: she perceives herself as its citizen, before considering herself as a "lady" or an ex-clergyman's daughter with wealthy and aristocratic connections" (41). Indeed, as Margaret insists that "if I live in a factory town, I must speak factory language when I want it" (*NS* 233), she attaches herself to the working class rather than the mill owners in an industrial town. However, when Bessy wonders why impoverished Margaret is invited to dinner by Thornton, Margaret explains to her that it is natural; "we are educated people and have lived amongst educated people. Is there anything so wonderful, in our being asked out to dinner by a man who owns himself inferior to my father by coming to him to be instructed?" (*NS* 147). Thus, Margaret is proud that her family are educated middle-class people and that the mill owner respects Mr Hale despite being economically impoverished in Milton. While Ingham has argued that Margaret's identity is fractured, I claim that Margaret's identity is hybrid, which is constructed by the pride of a middle-class lady and the sense of displacement of the marginalised outcast.

Margaret also has a mannish nature whose inclination is for power, even while she sympathises with the weak. She is attracted by the spirited and lively talk of the mill owners at Thornton's dinner:

> She liked the exultation in the sense of power which these Milton men had. It might be rather rampant in its display, and savour of boasting; but still they seemed to defy the old limits of possibility, in a kind of fine intoxication, caused by the recollection of what had been achieved, and what yet should be. (*NS* 162)

Although she objects to the mill owners' patriarchal authority over their workers, she is impressed with their powerful discussion about the difficulty of business and the strike by their workers. Their manner to "defy the old limits of possibility" inspires her in the marginalised space and urges her to think about 'what had been achieved' or 'what yet should be'. According to Ingham, "she can become a Trojan horse in the middle-class" (63). Indeed, Margaret, who has middle-class skills, is on familiar terms with Higgins, one of the union leaders, and intervenes in the class conflict between the employers and employees. When Thornton, who rises from poverty through his endeavour and "self-denial" (*NS* 85), looks down on the idle working-class, Margaret claims that the "two classes dependent on each other" (118) should abandon their hostility against the other and settle differences by way of discussion and compromises. When the workers attack Thornton's mill, Margaret goads him to speak with them face to face and tries to play the role of a mediator between Thornton and the workers. Although her impromptu intervention to save Thornton from the rioters reveals her mannish braveness and ability to take action, she regards her action of protecting him as maternal affection, which any woman embraces, to help a man whose life is at risk. While her action leads Thornton to misunderstand her feelings and propose to her, she is not aware of her feelings for him and, thus, rejects him, similar to how she rejected Lennox. She accuses him of being "blasphemous" and says that his whole manner "offends" her (*NS* 193), as her pride is wounded by the thought that he mistook her actions as arising from her feelings for him. To keep her pride as a middle-class woman, she takes up a cool, "haughty, and regal-proud" (*NS* 205) attitude to him. However, when she sees "the gleam of unshed tears in his eyes," she feels that "her proud dislike" turns into "something different and kinder" (*NS* 194).

In contrast to her refusal to Lennox, she feels remorseful about hurting Thornton's feeling and pride. While Margaret is too proud to accept his proposal, her kind sensitivity and maternal feelings lead her to sympathise with the weak and the injured. When Edith's boy loses his temper, Margaret exerts "a firm power which subdued him into peace" (*NS* 395), till he kisses her and falls asleep in her arms. Unlike Edith, who gives up on the treatment of her naughty child, Margaret considers a child's personality with maternal affection. Thus, Margaret has a hybrid nature of mannish courage and profound maternal affection.

To Mr Bell's surprise, after her residence in Milton for two years, Margaret comes to believe in the progress of commerce and decides to take up residence in northern Milton. When she was in southern Helstone, she abhorred of commerce and was prejudiced against the shoppy people. Even Mrs Hale chided her attitude: "You who were always accusing people of being shoppy at Helstone" (*NS* 87). Mr Hale also reprimands her for calling the Milton manufacturers tradespeople. Nevertheless, now that Margaret identifies herself as a resident in Milton, she responds to Mr Bell's disparagement of Milton people: "Milton people, I suspect, think Oxford men don't know how to move. It would be a very good thing if they mixed a little more" (*NS* 323). Mr Bell, an Oxford Fellow, also has a kind of prejudice against his native town—Milton—and argues that "as for sitting still, and learning from the past, or shaping out the future by faithful work done in a prophetic spirit…I don't believe there is a man in Milton who knows how to sit still; it is a great art" (*NS* 323). Margaret, the hybrid of *North and South*, ends up mediating between north and south. She suggests that it would do both the Milton manufacturers and Oxford men good if they "see a little more of the other" (*NS* 325). Thus, she recognises herself as an agent between *North and South*. As Mr Bell is a wealthy scholar with an immovable estate, including Thornton's factory and house, he does not understand why Milton's men strive for money. Thornton asserts that he does not strive for money:

> Mr Bell might speak of a little of leisure and serene enjoyment...; we do not look upon life as a time for enjoyment, but as a time for action and exertion. Our glory and our beauty arise out of our inward strength, which makes us victorious over material resistance, and over greater difficulties still. We are Teutonic up here in Darkshire in another way. (*NS* 326)

While he is proud of the strength of Darkshire men, Thornton's personality, which is typically characterised by diligence and humbleness, seems to change when he rejects his workers' demands for higher wages. Although Mr Bell judges Thornton as a man of dignity and vanity, Margaret does not evaluate him as being vain. Her vindication of Thornton demonstrates that her evaluation of Thornton has changed into a favourable one by doing him justice and leads Mr Bell to suspect Margaret's love for Thornton. Higgins, who begins to work at Thornton's mill based on Margaret's advice, realises that Thornton has two personalities: one is the typical master whom Higgins has known for long, and the other does not have a master's contemptuous nature and often visits Higgins to speak with him. Margaret's mediation between Thornton and Higgins allows Higgins to realise Thornton's true personality.

Similarly, Thornton's recognition of the miserable dinner at Higgins' house urges him to build the dining room for the workers at the site of his mill. Thornton purchases the provisions wholesale, employs a matron and cook and gives the workers the autonomy of the restaurant, where he is later invited to have lunch by his workers. Thornton follows Margaret's advice to talk with his workers; Thornton's consequent awareness regarding the frugal meal of the Higginses and his recognition that "cooking a good quantity of provisions together" will "save much money" (*NS* 353) represent his domesticity. In contrast to Mrs Thornton, who believes in materialism, he is also a hybrid of the masculine businessman and feminine domesticity. As Higgins notices that "he's two chaps" (*NS* 331), Thornton, who was a shop boy in his childhood, has the hybrid sensibility of the middle class and the working class akin to Margaret.

Margaret's visit to Helstone after her parents' death is arranged by Mr Bell, who wants to console his godchild and liberate her from the marginalised space in Mrs Shaw's house, where she has been treated like a servant since her parents' death. She is confined to Harley Street and has to take care of Edith's child while the other residents go out for social contact. However, it is not only the change of scenery offered by Helstone but also Thornton's misunderstanding that makes Margaret nervous and unstable. Confessing to Mr Bell that she lied to the inspector about her accompanying her brother to the station and that Thornton knows her lie, Margaret thinks it difficult to be free from her agony:

> I am so tired—so tired of being whirled on through all these phases of my life, in which nothing abides by me, no creature, no place; it is like the circle in which the victims of earthly passion eddy continually. I am in the mood in which women of another region take the veil. I

seek heavenly steadfastness in earthly monotony. (*NS* 390)

Margaret must have expected that Helstone would relieve her from her suffering, but its change deprives her of nostalgic enchantment. According to Patricia Ingham, Margaret "imagines herself 'whirled on' through all the phases of her life like sinful lovers in Dante, as if in 'the circle in which the victims of earthly passion eddy continually'" (68). As Ingham points out, she is "a divided self" between womanly "purity" and "a sense of sexual sin" (68). Although I agree that Margaret suffers from a divided self, I argue that her torment arises from her regrets that she told a lie and, thus, contravened the norms of a middle-class woman's decency, even though it was done to protect her brother from the police authority. Her torment is exacerbated by her knowledge that Thornton knows her lie and has mistaken her brother for her partner. She is divided between her proud self that has nothing to be blamed for with regard to her sexual purity and her guilty self, borne from having told a lie. However, Margaret's desire to escape from the torture of a divided self is temporary, and she recovers herself while walking across the common land with the morning sun: "the place was reinvested with the old enchanting atmosphere. The common sounds of life were more musical there than anywhere else in the whole world" (*NS* 391). Thus, Margaret's sense changes from negative to positive in one night. She is flexible rather than being a hybrid of positive and negative. As Wendy Parkins points out, "nostalgia is not a sign of a life-threatening disconnection from the modern world but rather an indication that Margaret sees herself as a modern subject who no longer belongs to the pastoral world of her childhood" (2009; 27). Margaret, the hybrid of South and North, is determined to live in the flux of the changing modern world while continuing to love her old home in Helstone, which is also not immune to change. Margaret accepts both the changes in herself and her home: "I too change perpetually" (*NS* 391).

As she accepts the change of her home into modernisation, she is ready to accept her changes within the flux of time. As Parkins argues, Margaret is situated "within processes of change" and recognises herself "as a historical subject" (2009; 28). In contrast to Margaret, Mr and Mrs Hale and Mr Bell cannot accept change. Mr Bell, whose father's orchard and birthplace were in Milton, refuses the change of Milton and deplores "the instability of all human things" (*NS* 379). Similarly, Mr and Mrs Hale cannot acclimatise to their new residence in northern Milton. All of them who could not accept the changes eventually retreat from the narrative. Margaret also affirms that "love for my species could never fill my heart to the utter exclusion of love for individuals" (*NS* 390). She regards personal relationships around her as more important than abstract love for humanity: "I must not think so much of how circumstances affect me myself, but how they affect others" (*NS* 391). She conceives her role is in modernity by realising her identity as a hybrid of place, class, and sensibility and ponders what she can do for others as an agent.

Later in the novel, after the death of her parents and Mr Bell, Margaret—the heir of Mr Bell's huge inheritance—goes to the seaside town of Cromer with Mr and Mrs Lennox and Aunt Shaw. Instead of travelling to Cadiz on the Spanish coast as she had originally intended, she compromises with them and goes to Cromer. However, this means that she has to give up the chance to meet Frederick, her brother, who married the daughter of a Spanish tradesperson and renounced his English citizenship. According to Robert Burroughs, besides work, the main reason for travel to the seaside in the eighteenth and early nineteenth centuries was "curative, but while the health benefits of a beach holiday continued to be claimed in resort advertising in the middle of the 1800s, increasingly the coast was identified as a place for pleasure" (13). While the aim of their visit to the seaside is to cure the depressed Margaret, who has experienced her intimate people's deaths in swift succession, she is left alone on the seashore. Unlike Mrs Shaw and Mr and Mrs Lennoxes' secular ways of spending seaside time, Margaret's occupation on the beach is devoted to her spiritual world. Staring at the waves, she muses on her past memories with her parents, Mr Bell, and Bessy. As Burroughs argues, people can have "religious and aesthetic contemplation" as well as "restfulness" on the shore (14). Margaret listens to the continuous sounds of the waves as if they were the eternal psalm by seeing that the ebb and flow reflect life and death. According to Wendy Parkins, "it is here that Margaret seeks both to historicise her past experience and determine her future occupations" (2009; 30). While Edith misapprehends Margaret's silence as her continuing to mope, the meditation on the beach "enabled Margaret to put events in their right places, as to origin and significance, both as regarded her past life and future" (*NS* 404). According to Burroughs, the sea's "vision of a new, or reformed, physical realm—a space without boundaries—perhaps resonates with Gaskell because of her conception of the waterfront as a space for personal renewal, including woman's discovery, or rediscovery, of their inner resources" (17). The restoration of Margaret's energy at Cromer is evinced by Henry Lennox's observation regarding her change and the effect of the sea. Margaret's effective spending of her time at Cromer contrasts with her stay at Heston with her parents early in the novel. While she visits Heston before Milton to help her invalid mother rest and recuperate, Margaret realises only "dreaminess in the rest" (*NS* 59) during a few days of interval between their hurried moving from Helstone to Milton. Margaret's "stroll down to the beach to breathe the sea-air" (*NS* 59), seeing "the white sail of a distant boat turning silver in some pale sunbeam", seemed as if she "could dream her life away in such luxury pensiveness" (60). Although a boat is compared to Lucy's life in *Villette*, a boat in Heston seems to be a distant existence from Margaret's present life before reaching Milton. In reality, Margaret neither longs for "the past" nor visualises "the future" in Heston, but she has to think about "her present" (*NS* 60) life. According to Burroughs, "Margaret's experience of Heston is testament to the modern tourist beach's ability to de-materialise experience and erase history, be it personal or social, in the promotion of indolent pleasure" (19). However, Margaret cannot afford the ordinary tourist's pleasure during her stay in Heston as she has to plan her new residence in Milton without indulging in a 'luxury' pastime. In contrast to her contemplation in Cromer, she undergoes no development in character at Heston; however, Margaret's observation of the difference between the northern and southern shores prepares her for Northern Milton. In Cromer, Margaret reflects upon her past and makes clear decisions regarding her future by placing herself in modernity. According to Marshall Berman, "the ideas of modernization and modernism emerge and unfold…from the sense of living in two worlds simultaneously…materially and spiritually" (17). Indeed, Margaret embraces the sense of living in the material environment and begins to contemplate practical questions, such as how to manage Mr Bell's inheritance. Simultaneously, she lives in the spiritual world, where she is annoyed by questions about how she intends to live as an independent woman. She discovers her inner ability: "Margaret fulfilled one of her sea-side resolves, and took her life into her own hands" (*NS* 406). Her "solemn hours of thought" (*NS* 406) in Cromer liberates her from Aunt Shaw's laws and allows her to feel responsible for her own life: "she tried to settle that most difficult problem for women, how much was to be utterly merged in obedience to authority, and how much might be set apart for freedom in working" (*NS* 406). Margaret's manner is a hybrid of the independence and obedience of the Victorian age. Acquiring Mr Bell's inheritance, Margaret acknowledges "her right to follow her own ideas of duty" and decides to get her own way as "a strong-minded woman" (*NS* 406). Margret has an "innate sense of oppression" (*NS* 193), which Thornton is aware of. Unlike Mrs Shaw and Edith, who have a domestic quality, Margaret has a short "temper", "quick perception", and "over-lively imagination"; nevertheless, she has lovely "childlike sweetness of heart" (*NS* 406). Thus, Margaret identifies herself as an independent-minded woman with a strong mind. According to Parkins, "she [Margaret] takes on a role as philanthropist or slum visitor, an emerging occupation for middle-class women, in the second half of the nineteenth century" (2009; 31). Certainly, judging from Edith's criticism about Margaret's ramblings in Milton's slum, middle-class women had to have a strong mind to carry out philanthropic activities in the wretched places. However, Margaret regards her association with the Higginses and the other working-class people as friendships based on her human interest rather than philanthropic visits. Irrespective of the size of her fortune, she has no class boundary because her sensibility is a hybrid of the middle class and working class.

In the last scene of the novel, we see the destruction of the boundaries of gender, age, and the private and the public in aunt Shaw's typical upper-middle-class house. Edith tries to silence her little boy in the back drawing room, where Margaret and Lennox hold the conference. Thus, while the adults talk about business matters, a child is not confined to the nursery by the nurse. As children, Margaret and Edith were separated from adults into the nursery by "the notion of protectionism" (222), which Andrea Kaston Tange points out. Tange argues that the children had to stay in the nursery "except when appearing at prescribed times, carefully groomed, and on 'best behaviour' downstairs" (222). Lennox complains of the disturbance caused by Edith and her child: "I will try, when I marry, to look out for a young lady who has a knowledge of the management of children" (*NS* 423). Traditional and shrewd Lennox seems to recognise that Margaret's effect deprives Harley Street of the traditional norms of middle-class and gives up on his attempts to marry Margaret. Even Lennox does not feel strange when he warns Edith: "the only detail I want you to understand is, to let us have the back drawing-room undisturbed, as it was today" (*NS* 423).

The back drawing room is quite a private room, linked to the feminine Edith at the beginning of the novel. According to Divya Athmanathan, "his remarks illustrate the changes wrought onto the homogeneous nature of the back drawing-room of the opening scene. The space permeated by femininity has been expanded to include the discourse of business affairs" (49). Indeed, to discuss the land which Thornton rents from Margaret, she brings the public affairs, such as investments, leases, and value of land into the private back drawing room, and the drawing room is transformed into a hybrid space of the private and the public. Besides, Margaret suggests that Thornton should take her eighteen thousand and fifty-seven pounds lying unused in the bank at a higher interest than the bank to help his distressed factory. As Athmanathan points out, "Margaret's business proposal and Thornton's marriage proposal further establish the back drawing-room as a space capable of allowing multiple interests to flourish" (51). Thus, Margaret's hybrid sensibility and position affect the people around her as she moves from South to North, transforming her space including herself. As Tim Cresswell argues that "identities are produced and performed through mobility" (44), Margaret's identity transforms from a private philanthropist in the South into a public philanthropic businesswoman in the North. In the hybrid of the public and private space, the hybrid sensibilities of Margaret and Thornton resonate with one another. Margaret, a hybrid of northern and southern culture, has the opportunity to be a social and political hybrid through her marriage to a manufacturer in Milton. As Homi Bhabha argues, "the cultural hybridity gives rise to something different, something new and unrecognizable, a new area of negotiation of meaning and representation" (211). Margaret, placing herself in the flux of the changing society in modernity, identifies herself as a changing self who has a hybrid sensibility and conception and as the mediator of linking the different cultures, classes and spaces, while challenging the traditional norm of society.

Conclusion

This study has explored how the protagonists' mobility in the selected Victorian novels—*Jane Eyre*, *Villette*, and *North and South*—operates to produce their space and identity. Nineteenth-century England witnessed a transport revolution caused by technological advancements, and experienced extensive social, economic, and cultural shifts including industrialisation, urbanisation, and an increasingly mobile population. In such an epoch, which aimed for modernity, women, especially middle-class women, were confined to the social norms such as the segregation of gender, class, and space. As we have seen, Charlotte Brontë and Elizabeth Gaskell were keenly interested in gendered dichotomies and social shifts and deliberately unearthed the new relationship between women and their space, between their mobility and their inner space including their identity in their literal space. This study has examined what the protagonists in their novels experience through their mobility in a changing society, and how their perception through such mobility affects their inner space and realises their self and identity.

As is explored herein, since Henri Lefevre claimed in his work, *The Production of Space* (1974), that space is a social product which always interacts with social practices and forces, 'space' has attracted the feminist geographers' interest. Linda McDowell argues that advanced industrial societies produce several ways in which male superiority and control are constructed and enforced. Such a hierarchical relationship shaped a discourse of spatial usages based on gender and class norms, the ideology of "separate spheres" between the public and the private, between inside and outside, which restricted the activities of middle-class women in the Victorian age. However, Judith Butler's argument that the fragilities of the boundaries of the assigned space and the traditional norm provide women with the possibility to deviate from them. Additionally, Doreen Massey's claim that space is always under construction, involving shifts motivated this study to trace the protagonists' trial to transgress from traditional norms and to build new space.

In addition to these significant arguments about space, this study is based on the theories of mobility and modernity. Recently, the scholars on sociology and geography have focused on "mobility" as a new methodology to examine what happens to people and things and what they experience in spaces between places. As documented in previous chapters, John Urry argues mobility does not only mean physical or geographical movements but one's delicate movements in social positions and crowd's movements out of control. Indeed, Jane Eyre, Lucy Snow, and Margaret Hale experience some kinds of mobility, not only geographical movement but also shifts of social positions; in the case of Margaret, she is involved in the mob. According to Ingrid Horrocks, mobility enables us to trace the meanings, metaphors, and ideologies attached to the movements of people and things. Tim Creswell also argues that human mobility is not just about travelling from one place to another, it is socially produced motion which means an irreducibly embodied experience of humans. Thus, like space, mobility is produced socially and represents "meaningful and laden with power" (Cresswell 9) connotations. While this study regards walking as the most significant means of mobility for heroines to produce space, the combination of walking, coaches, railways, and ships offers them various opportunities for connection, transgression, and metaphors and for their embracing or rejecting modernity.

This study has demonstrated that the protagonists experience modernity through their mobility. As Anthony Giddens claims, modernity is "the industrialised world" which connects to capitalism, "established first of all in post-feudal Europe" (15), the centre of which was Victorian-era England. Jane, Lucy, and Margaret are voluntarily or involuntarily involved in modernity, which brings about industrialisation and urbanisation, affecting the women's roles and gender identities. While walking is regarded as a form of premodern mobility, the protagonists in the selected novels are not always detached from the modernised world when they walk in commercial and merchant cities, manufacturing towns, cosmopolitan cities, and institutions within a postal network, embracing the feeling of road improvements, disciplinary mechanisms, and national community. By setting their narratives at a turning point in the history of transport, Brontë and Gaskell illustrate that the modern technology opened up women's new perspectives to space and time. Journeys by coach, ship, and rail enable the protagonists to undertake long-distance travel and experience new environments. However, comfortable and convenient modern transportation systems sometimes become harsh and cruel methods of mobility, providing Jane, Lucy, and Margaret with feelings of sudden dislocation or detachment from familiar places. Thus, modern mobility has expanded the range of women's access to new places and makes them experience new perception of the changing times and space they traverse.

Modernity is more than just technological development, as Marshall Berman argues, "to find ourselves in an environment that promise us adventure, power, joy, growth, transformation of ourselves and the world" (15), but, simultaneously, we acknowledge that we are in the circumstances threatening to destroy everything we have, know, and what we are. While modernity, as Marshall Berman claims, transgresses all boundaries of geography, ethnicity, class, nationality, region, and ideology, "modernity...produces difference, and exclusion and marginalisation" (Giddens 6). This study has traced how the protagonists cross the various boundaries, how they negotiate with the difficulties, and how they overcome marginalisation.

Focusing on walking as the basic means of the protagonists' mobility, this study has examined the new and changing relationship between women and space: the mobile protagonists' experienced and embodied space in a modernising society. While walking for leisure was a privilege only for middle-class men in the eighteenth century, women's mobility did not become more acceptable and facile until the nineteenth century. In *Jane Eyre*, *Villette*, and *North and South*, the female protagonists are frequent travellers on foot: they walk for pleasure, health, work, necessity, freedom, and sometimes without purposes and destinations. Jane Eyre enjoys walking for the first time when she rambles in the wood all day long near the Lowood School. While poor sick girls are dying in the institution, Jane, liberated from surveillance, rules, and restrictions, goes out of the school to walk freely towards her favourite spot to dine in, enjoying the communication with nature. Walking stimulates her healthy appetite and improves her physical condition, which she felt was inferior to that of the Reed children at Gateshead Hall. While the child Lucy Snow loved walking along a quiet street with an antique atmosphere in Bretton, twenty-three-year-old Lucy finds herself excited about walking along the busy and bustling streets in London, the metropolitan city. This is because she finds herself freed from her confinement within Miss Marchmont's house and the small hamlet in the middle of England. Her walk in the vibrant city provides her with a healthy appetite and makes her feel an affinity with the seriousness of the capitalist modernity. Returning to her rural hometown, Helstone, Margret Hale is delighted to walk freely without interference of her aunt, who insists that middle-class daughters should be accompanied by a footman. Not caring about her father's modest economy which cannot afford a horse or a carriage, she walks with joy crushing herbs underfoot in the forest and enjoys communicating with the people in the cottages. While her walk in the country is linked to her spontaneous philanthropic spirit, she also wants to escape from the confinement of the parsonage where her mother complains about their humble life. Thus, in the three selected novels, walking itself becomes an adventure for the female protagonists, providing them with opportunities to enjoy freedom, independence, communication with nature, and self-discovery. Furthermore, throughout their walks, Jane, Lucy, and Margaret begin a conversation with not only their own bodies but also inner space. Refusing to be restricted inside a house, they try to make contact with the outer world and achieve self-fulfilment through movement from one place to another negotiating with or resisting gender and class norms.

As Tim Creswell argues, identities are created, produced, and performed through mobility. Based on this suggestion, I have explored the mobile protagonists' walking or mobility by some kinds of transportation, which leads to a deeper appreciation of the relationship among women, space, and identity. As demonstrated in earlier chapters, Jane, Lucy, and Margaret's socially marginalised position and uncategorised nature allow them to cut across all boundaries that shaped the idea of 'proper' middle-class lady, which means that they experience modern environments. As an abandoned child, Jane embarks on a journey alone by coach to Lowood Institution and an adult Jane wanders in the wilderness of the moorland as a nameless vagrant. Lucy crosses the sea by ship to search for a job after losing her position as Miss Marchmont's nurse and companion. After her father's resignation from his position as a clergyman, Margaret is no longer a daughter in Helstone parsonage, adapting herself in a new environment by building friendships with the family of factory workers in northern-Milton. Throughout their mobility, the protagonists learn how to speak effectively, that is, their own speech to create their identity. Michel Foucault's notion of "heterotopia" enabled me to explore the sites of middle-class women's struggle to discover or build identity. Not following the ordinary regulations of time and space, space of heterotopia such as a mirror, theatre, festival, museum, and ship creates an original space that exposes the real feature by being "represented, contested, and inverted" (Foucault 239, 1977). As I have discussed, heterotopic spaces which belong to modernity function as important spaces for the protagonists to not only recognise and develop their original nature and character, but also reassume or build identity.

In *Jane Eyre*, the child Jane has to walk two miles from Lowood School to the church every Sunday during winter with other poor girls. Forcing girls disciplined and controlled march, Lowood School is a kind of modern institution associated with disciplinary mechanisms, as Foucault highlights. When typhus transformed Lowood into a hospital isolated from society, situated "outside of all spaces" (Foucault 239, 1977), a heterotopic space, Jane is absorbed in her free walk and returns to face the death of her closest friend, Helen. In contrast to Helen, who believes in God and goes to Heaven, Jane begins her journey seeking independence and happiness in this world.

Jane's inclination for freedom in walking nurtured in the wood close to Lowood has been embedded in her and motivates her to depart to a new place ever after. Eighteen-year-old Jane opens the window of Lowood, desiring to go along the road leading her to an unfamiliar world. Eager for adventure, change, and stimulus, Jane is glad that her new workplace, Thornfield Hall, is near Milton, a large manufacturing town with bustling lives and movements. At Thornfield, Jane never misses the opportunity to go outside by voluntarily going on an errand to walk two miles to the post office. Her helping and supporting Rochester on her way alludes to the possibility that their positions within the gendered power structure are reversed. Thus, her walking contributes to the development of the narrative. Bored of monotonous life with Adel and Mrs Fairfax, Jane, seeking adventure, walks backwards and forwards along the corridor of the third storey, suspecting the sound of someone's murmur. Indeed, Jane is a woman who lives in modernity which offers her adventure, joy, and transformation of herself and the world around her. While she learns repression, manner, and moderate speech appropriate to a lady in Lowood, Jane rejects to obey Rochester's order to say something to please him. Rochester is more amazed at her refusal showing her challenge to patriarchy than upset and notices her power of words. Her words associated with her identity attracts him, as Lesa Scholl highlights that "language is tied to identity" (101). Thus, while Jane's speech as well as walking often functions to develop a romantic relationship with Rochester at Thornfield, their spatial division before their wedding connotes their disunity. The contrast between Jane in liminal space such as corridors and Rochester in the master's dining room reserving his wine, and that between Jane waiting for his return in the garden and Rochester going thirty miles away from the house on business indicate that the boundary of class and gender segregations is drawn both inside and outside the house. The drive by Rochester's new coach to Milton also makes Jane uncomfortable, as it indicates the disparity in social position between them.

Jane's wandering on the moorland with no money signifies her transgression of the middle-class women's ideals. Set down from the coach of the social network and becoming outcast from the human community, she clings to nature and feels restful in the natural landscape for a while. During her roaming, losing her identity as a middle-class woman, a governess, and even her name, Jane's body is centred in her space; like an animal, she sleeps on the grass and walks with an awareness of her pains of foot and limbs and hunger. However, recognising that she cannot live in nature by herself, she heads to the nearby village as a nobody. When Jane is on the verge of becoming a fallen woman, she is led to her relative's home, Moor House, at which point she returns to the human community. Finding a congeniality of tastes, sentiments, and principles between herself and the Rivers sisters, Jane reaffirms what she is and what she really wants to become, assimilating herself in their middle-class life and house. Moor House serves as a proving ground for Jane to recover her domesticity before returning to Rochester's residence. While St John offers her the position of the schoolmistress of the village, she abandons the job as soon as she accepts the inheritance. She rejects his proposal that she should accompany him to India as a missionary wife. Thus, Jane retreats from the public space and does not go across the boundary of geography. Indeed, Jane's radical claim and desire for adventure and stimulus seen in Lowood and Thornfield disappear, and her reiterated renovation from her transgression, which originated from her awareness of the child Jane's reflection of "revolted slave" (*JE* 18) in the mirror at the red-room in Gateshead, returns her to an independent middle-class woman with her own original taste and power of words. Thus, as Mathieson argues, while Jane deviates from "the appropriate social order of female mobility" (55), she eventually recovers her feminine decency as a middle-class woman. Moor House sequestered from society and surrounded by nature, and quiet and modest pastoral life become Jane's ideal. At the end of narrative, Jane, like the "messenger-pigeon flying home" (*JE* 487), returns to Rochester's residence in Ferndean, which is similar to Moor House, sequestered from society. She recognises that through mobility, she reaches her ideal home where she enjoys freedom, equality, and peace of mind without the segregation of gender and class and patriarchal rules with a blind and maimed husband.

Jane's walking provides her with not only the opportunity to feel freedom and enjoy communicating with nature but also the perception of difficulties of forced discipline and the harshness of nature. Jane's mobility clarifies that her end of journey is not a modernised, public, and urban city life but a rural, private, and static life. For Jane, the stagecoach is not a comfortable means of transportation but rather a troublesome one that ruthlessly brings her from one place to another unfamiliar place and causes her to become uneasy or lose something. Compared with walking, stagecoach travel only makes Jane conscious of time and distance. Her wandering on the moorland reveals that middle-class women do not have the space to live off the beaten track, outside of human society. Jane's mobility offers her the limited human relationship including the meeting with Rochester, the Revers family, and the people in Lowood. Unlike Margret in *North and South* or Lucy in *Villette*, Jane scarcely mingles with people from different classes, nor voyages across the sea. We have to remember Anthony Giddens' argument that "a person's identity is…in the capacity to keep a particular narrative going" (54) when we notice that Jane is about to finish her story at the end of the novel: "My tale draws to its close" (*JE* 519). Her announcement of resignation from the narrative signifies that she will live a static life without change, aloof from modernity. Jane, recovered by the Rivers sisters' care, notices that Moor House is her ideal home, which awakens her nostalgia and identity as a middle-class woman. Ferndean is appropriate as Jane's last home with the blind Rochester, sequestered from the bustling society, away from the temptation, danger, and materialism of modernity that she knows exerted a corrupting influence on the young Rochester. As illustrated by the fact that she takes his hand and serves as his prop and guide, she creates a self-centred space without segregation of gender and class and restriction by patriarchy.

As Lucy Morrison argues, Lucy Snowe in *Villette* is a peripatetic traveller who walks around without purpose. Lucy's walking differs from Margaret's in *North and South* and Jane's in *Jane Eyre* in that she has no destinations or necessities. Lucy often states that her nature is inactive and does not seek sudden changes or adventures; however, her walking provokes her innate nature and urges her to undertake daring deeds. Accidentally hearing the unreliable story that many British women work as nurses in foreign families, she decides to leave the small hamlet and test her ability abroad. Boarding a ship, Lucy by chance hears Ginebra's story that Madame Beck in Villette is seeking an English governess, which urges Lucy to head for Villette, a town completely unfamiliar to her. Thus, Lucy's deeds are often very reckless and thoughtless. Her daring deeds seem to stem from her rootlessness and homelessness. She says, "I had nothing to lose...If I failed in what I now designed to undertake, who, save myself, would suffer?...I had no home...then, who would weep?" (*V* 49–50). Her remark indicates that she does not regard even Mrs Bretton, her godmother, or John, her son, as her family. In *Villette*, the protagonist's precarious and ambiguous nature as an orphaned and homeless woman allow her to walk freely and independently, which consequently enables her to transgress the boundaries of gender and class.

The development of a new mobile culture in the nineteenth century became an important turning point, especially for marginalised middle-class women who did not have money, family, and home. In *Villette*, the housekeeper who was previously Lucy's nurse tells her that many English women work in foreign countries as nurses. This suggests that in nineteenth-century Britain, many women no longer stayed at home and voluntarily or involuntarily embarked on a journey seeking financial independence. Madame Beck remarks that "it is only English girls who can thus be trusted to travel alone" (*V* 53), which represents Brontë's esteem for English women's courageous mobility despite hardships and changing society which tolerates women travelling unaccompanied. Seeking a job, Lucy travels across the sea, the boundary between England and the continent. While other passengers suffer from seasickness, a risk of modernity (Matheson 99), Lucy enjoys liberty in the sea breeze on deck. She gets seasick only when she blames herself for having too many expectations for a life in a new world. Indeed, on reaching Labassecour, she feels the foreign country's hostile rejection from the cold air and uneasiness through being chased by two unknown men. However, the modernised environments of Villette make Lucy feel more secure. Her trunk is misplaced during the coach journey, but is later forwarded to her. When the coach arrives at the town, she notices that soldiers are stationed at the bureau to protect the safety of the town. Thus, unlike Jane, who was unexpectedly set down by coach in the moorland and lost all her property, Lucy is not totally cast out from the communal networked nation. Later, Lucy even feels a sense of superiority when she drives in a carriage with the Brettons to the theatre and the concert hall, observing the street full of shops and people. Unlike in *Jane Eyre*, modern transportation functions as means for the protagonist to move from one place to another not only for necessity but also for pleasure and entertainment.

In *Villette*, the protagonist's walking serves as a narrative strategy for plot development; however, it also enables Lucy to discover herself and have psychological illusions about her future, personal relationship, and the space around her. In London, Lucy relishes her liberty by escaping from confinement for the first time. While fourteen-year-old Lucy loves quiet and antique atmosphere of Bretton, adult Lucy realises her inclination for a modern, metropolitan city during her stay in London. Her long and aimless walk in the city stimulates her healthy appetite and makes her comfortably fatigued. Furthermore, she is confident about walking alone across crossings and along busy streets in the flood of the crowd. Thus, unlike Jane, Lucy enjoys her physical and psychological journey both in rural and urban areas. However, on arrival in London, she experiences culture shock; when she alights from the stagecoach, she cannot understand the conversation between the cabmen and other passengers, which makes her feel as if she were in ancient Babylon. However, Lucy in London demonstrates her ability to assimilate herself into modernised environments through her walking in the city. Going up the orbed mass of St. Paul's Dome, she recognises her place on the cosmic scale and shows that she is ready for crossing the sea, crossing any boundary.

Lucy's free walk is associated with her personal pleasure. While she walks in the flood of the crowd, she keeps her mind distanced from others, and therefore, she can enjoy being totally alone. In Villette, Lucy takes herself a step closer towards the public sphere by working as an English teacher at the girls' school. Unlike in London, where she was merely an observer of the bustling city life, she is involved in the educational space. However, feeling confinement under Madame Beck's surveillance and espionage, Lucy finds pleasure in walking by herself along the secret alley in the school garden, which is situated between the girls' school and boys' school. Her preference for the alley connotes her identity of in-betweenness. The narrow path allows her to listen to the sounds of people walking along the street for entertainment and feel the energy of the cosmopolitan city that is involved in modernity. Lucy starts to enjoy walking outside the school after she reunites with the Bretton family. Lucy has the opportunity to visit art museums and theatres, but even when she is in the museum, she enjoys walking alone to examine the pictures quietly by herself. In the art museum, a heterotopic space accumulating time, which confines the paintings depicted by male artists of all times in one place, Lucy examines, questions, and inverts the femininity, tradition, and values that have been assigned to women throughout history. In the theatre, she is impressed by Vashti, whose transgressive performance is associated with modernity. Lucy's walking in heterotopias evokes her inner consciousness and opposition to patriarchy. Lucy's experience of performing on stage in a school play requires her to decide how to behave and what to wear metaphorically. As Anthony Giddens argues, modernity consistently asks us how we live, how we behave, speak, eat, and wear, day by day, and we have to make our choice one by one (14). In the school play, Lucy immediately decides how to behave and what to wear as is suitable for her role, insisting that she should wear both women's and men's clothes. As Giddens' theory suggests, this interpretation through questions and answers leads Lucy to her perception of identity of in-betweenness, and the discovery of her own voice. Dr John Bretton, a kind English gentleman, often helps Lucy to expand the range of her access to new places. He takes her not only to the museums but also to the Basse-Ville, a poor and crowded district in the town, which provides her with more knowledge about the town. Having a strong, independent mind, she gradually comes to realise that she does not need his help. She can prevent him from entering her private alley. On the festival night, she keeps her distance from the Brettons and the de Bassompierres, and Dr John accepts her refusal to accompany them. Thus, Lucy prefers walking alone to getting involved in any community or unity. Walking allows her freedom, independence, and transgressive mobility, which offers her self-discovery.

Affected by opium in the festival, Lucy's enthusiastic walking allows her to trace the history of Labassecour. According to Michel Foucault, festivals are the external space linked to "time in its most flowing, transitory, precarious aspects" and people can experience the rediscovery of "time" in them (1998; 242). Walking on festival night, Lucy remembers its history that it honours citizens and patriots who died for freedom and rights. However, she notices the contrast between the seriousness of the history and the frivolous appearance of the festival. Lucy's second visit to the Basse-Ville also offers her a better understanding of the history of the town; she witnesses the contrast between its former wealth supported by flourishing business and its current ruinous poverty. Lucy's familiarity with the town of Villette indicates that she comes to take root in the soil of Villette, which will be her final abode, while her geographical knowledge of Bretton was limited. Although she notices Madame Walravens' malicious entrapment to revive her plantation, Lucy neither stops Paul Emanuel's departure nor lets her "life-boat" (*V* 181) rescue him. Indeed, Lucy is involved in modernity in that her immigration offers her assimilation into the foreign country, but simultaneously, her inner perception refuses Paul's success in the plantation for ends of selfishness of Rome and Madame Walravens, and she accepts the shipwreck in which Paul is involved, the risk of modernity.

Lucy's last walk, covering a good distance into Faubourg with M. Paul, leads her to her home and school that she has aspired to since she left England. Thus, Lucy, an immigrant to Villette, finally gains her own space and can mingle with the residents in the cosmopolitan town of Villette: "these companies are pedestrians, make little noise, and are soon gone" (*V* 469). However, throughout her walking, she displays her preference for private spaces. I argue that such an inclination to be alone makes Lucy a distanced observer and a foreigner both in Britain and Villette. Lucy, the narrator, stops her narrative by saying, "[H]ere pause: pause at once. There is enough said. Trouble no quiet, kind heart; leave sunny imaginations hope" (*V* 496). This ending strongly suggests Paul's death. However, despite its pessimistic tone, unlike *Jane Eyre*, the open ending promises that Lucy's story still continues, and we know that she will live until her hair becomes "white, under a white cap, like snow beneath snow" (*V* 45) and her school, which was modelled on Madame Beck's boarding school, will also bring her a prosperous and successful life in modernity. As pupils from both burgher and higher classes study together in Lucy's school, it is beyond the class boundaries. Among the mobile heroines in the three selected novels, Lucy experiences the most dynamic geographical movement by voyaging to an unknown foreign country. With neither a letter of recommendation nor an acquaintance in this new world, Lucy boldly jumps into a completely new environment. Unlike Jane who never forgets Rochester during her roaming, and Margaret, who is reminiscent of her hometown, Lucy hardly looks back over her home, England, in the narrative, which indicates that she is exclusively interested in how she will live a life in the future, changing society, and modernising world.

Margaret Hale in *North and South* is an original pedestrian. As with Jane and Lucy, walking reveals the protagonist's inclination for freedom, nature, and independence. More importantly, walking is a significant communication tool for Margaret to make a connection with someone or something. At first, Margaret is scared by unfamiliar factory workers' bald faces, loud laugh, and jest in the industrial town of Milton. Her casual meeting with Higgins and his daughter, Bessy, allows her to have a human interest, which motivates her to build new relationships with new people. Adapting her charitable attitude to fit the regional circumstances of Milton, such as her friendship with Bessy, Margaret succeeds in cultivating a good human relationship with the Higginses and comes to exchange opinions with them in person. Thus, since her meeting with the Higginses, Milton becomes a habitable space for Margaret; she begins to be accustomed to walking along the streets of the industrial town and the community of inhabitants.

As Lesa Scholl highlights, Margaret adapts and belongs to the other groups by speaking like them. Using the peculiar dialect and words of the villagers in Helstone and those of working-class people in Milton,

Conclusion

Margaret's perception of her identity is not confined to a middle-class one, namely she has a hybrid nature, sensibility, and position. In addition to her ability of verbal communication, Margaret's mobility also serves to mingle with people in a new environment. At their first meeting, Margaret walks at a slow pace to talk intimately with the Higgins family, which enables her to notice Bessy's feeble legs owing to her illness. After Bessy's death, Margaret invites Higgins to her house to console him, while the middle-class people did not invite the working-class people. During their walk to Crampton, although she worries about her father's reaction, she never forgets to pay delicate attention to Higgins' distress caused by his daughter's death. Later, she steps into Boucher's house to inform his wife of his death while her father and Higgins hesitate to do so. Thus, Margaret's mobility, which connects with her kind nature, removes the class boundaries between herself and others. She not only takes on Mr. Hale's role as a clergyman, but also bravely faces the modernising environments that include risks. Although she was unaware of the struggle between the manufacturers and the workers in the country, she is involved in the dangerous riot, which is brought about by capital modernity, in the industrial town.

Margaret's private association with both working people and their master, Thornton, makes her position ambiguous. That is, she is not regulated by the middle-class norm that obeys the dichotomy of public/private spheres and segregations of classes. Through the conversation with the Higginses, Margaret learns about the factory, strike, and union, and other modern problems. Her knowledge about commerce gained via the argument with Thornton and factory situations makes her privileged compared to other middle-class women in Milton. Escaping from women's conversation about trivial things at Mrs Thornton's dinner party, Margaret is pleased to understand the manufacturers' discussion on "something larger and grander" (*NS* 162): manufacturing activities, trade, and confrontation with the workers. Thus, Margaret is a hybrid of a lady and gentleman. Later, involved in the industrial riot, thanks to her perception of the workers' difficult circumstances, Margaret can act bravely in the public sphere, even though she cannot play the perfect role of mediator between two classes. Margaret displays her prejudice against manufacturers by calling them shoppy people, and this was because she had never interacted with them when she stayed in Mrs Shaw's house in London. Her observation that the lack of interaction between the employer and their employees in Milton causes their conflict urges Thornton to speak with his workers face-to-face when the rioters attack his house. Compared with the women trembling in the drawing room of Thornton's house, Margaret demonstrates her mobile ability and courage to be involved in the industrial dispute by tearing the bonnet to listen to Thornton talk from the window, rushing downstairs, and going out of the house to stand between the angry workers and Thornton. Margaret's attendance in her mother's funeral against the middle-class norm in the Victorian era also represents her resolute attitude.

Giddens claims that "modernity is a risk culture" (3) and that while "modernity reduces the overall risks of certain areas and modes of life", it simultaneously "introduces new risk parameters largely or completely unknown to previous eras" (4). In *North and South*, the railway network reveals several modern problems and risks that nineteenth-century British people experienced. The fast and punctual train inexorably wrenches the Hale family from their beloved hometown. The train's punctuality makes Margaret nervous during her travel from London to Helstone with Mr Bell, and he takes out insurance against train accidents for her. Leonards' death caused by falling off a platform represents new risks and dangers around the railway. Although the railroad is sometimes associated with the image of uneasy transportation, Margaret comes to appreciate its comfort and convenience as modern transportation. The train drives Margaret home safely when she is so terrified and exhausted by Leonards' chase that she cannot walk herself. Informed that Mr Bell is critically ill, she insists that she must go to Oxford by rail by herself. When her father passed away at Oxford, she was too devastated to travel to Oxford by train. This time, however, she never wants to miss a chance to see Mr Bell and she takes the next train accompanied by Captain Lenox. Thus, Margaret comes to appreciate the railroad journey that offers her fast and long-distance travel.

Margaret's walking usually has a destination and purpose, such as running an errand for her parents or providing philanthropic aid. These actions are not observed in the narratives of Jane and Lucy, who are orphans. Margaret begins to walk for herself when she becomes parentless and visits Helstone. The train bound for the south offers her the same pastoral landscape as she saw three years ago, letting her feel as if she were a refugee from the modernised industrial city. While the unchanging scenery from the fly at first annoys her in comparison to her changed circumstances, her recognition of the change in the village and its inhabitants depresses her. However, walking with Mr Bell around the village, Margaret admits that the change and improvement is necessary to modernise society. Walking to the garden of the Vicarage by herself allows her to feel the possibility of her own change. The contemplation at the seaside of Cromer after acquiring Mr Bell's inheritance allows her to compartmentalise the past tragic events in their right places to face the present and the future. As Berman argues that modernisation emerges from the sense of living in two worlds of materials and spirit (17), Margaret recognises how she should use her money (Mr Bell's inheritance) and how she will live as an independent woman in modernity. Acknowledging her innate strength and responsibility, she insists that she has got her own way and will buy her dresses for herself. Thus, she reveals her independence of the regulation of middle-class women assigned by Victorian society. The narrative ends with Margaret and Thornton's discussion about declaring their upcoming marriage to their relatives in the back drawing room. Their conversation about their marriage as well as business represents that the drawing room, which was linked to feminine Edith, is transformed into a hybrid space of the private and the public. Margaret's future involvement in the activities of Milton, a fast-growing manufacturing town, signifies her position as an independent woman in modernity.

In the three novels, the protagonists' walking is connected with the changing environments of the Victorian age, spaces where gender and class politics and the sense of regional differences are involved. While middle-class women's walking is often subject to restrictions, it allows them to challenge the dichotomy of male/female and public/private spheres. Furthermore, their deviation from the Victorian norms creates their own space where they can act on their own judgement. While Charlotte Mathieson argues that Jane returns to a domestic national order "on the condition of the stasis of domesticity" (55), she also changes from a marginalised governess into a self-centred hostess who guides her husband by gaining family connections with the Rivers family and an inheritance from her uncle. Similarly, Lucy perceives her "placelessness" and marginalised situation as a shadow-like figure in both England and Villette; however, as Liana F. Piehler argues, her awareness of her inner passion and desire at heterotopic sites such as a theatre and gallery transforms her into "her height of self-achievement" (69). She no longer worries about how other people think of her by creating a physically and mentally self-centred space as a self-confident mistress of a girls' boarding school, which she expands next to the home M. Paul prepared. Although her school flourishes, she will not relinquish the house filled with his memory. As Linda McDowell, referring to Bachelard's view, argues, "'the house and dwelling' function 'as a storehouse of memories'" (72). Lucy inhabits and works between the house, which is filled with M. Paul's masculine memory, and her girls' boarding school, recognising herself as in-betweenness. In contrast to Jane, who retreats to her private space, Lucy achieves both spheres of business/home and the public/private in the modern city. Margaret in *North and South*, who originally has a hybrid nature that combines a middle-class woman's pride and the familiar easiness of the servants, changes from a daughter of the clergyman in the country into a margin-alised woman in the city. Crossing the boundaries of classes, regions, and the dichotomy of private and public spheres, Margaret tries to mediate the modern problems between the masters and workers in the industrial city. At the end of the narrative, the Shaws' private back drawing room transforms into the business space where Margaret negotiates with Thornton and, simultaneously functions as a private space where she accepts his proposal. Thus, in the last scene, Gaskell skilfully creates the hybrid space of the private/public. We see that neither Margaret nor Thornton adheres to a Victorian ideology, and Margaret, a woman with a flexible sense, has the courage to accept her changes in the changing modern society.

I argue that Jane Eyre, Lucy Snowe, and Margaret Hale, mobile protagonists deliberately characterised by Charlotte Brontë and

Elizabeth Gaskell, overcome their displacement, explore and create their own dynamic space, and act independently in the restricted society. As demonstrated in previous chapters, the selected three novels illustrate that space, mobility, and identity interrelate and interact with each other flexibly in a modernised world which accepts shifts and changes constantly. Mobility allows the protagonists to trace the expansion of middle-class women's field of activities. The deviations of their spatial usages from gender and class norms signify the fragility of social space, especially the space that Victorian society constructed, as Doreen Massey points out that space is "always under construction" and accompanies "shifts" (24). The regulation imposed on the protagonists do not discourage them from embarking on a journey for their new space. Through their physical and psychological journey, Jane, Lucy, and Margaret encounter new people and culture, and come to practice their own speech, and achieve their identities and space to belong to, which indicates that they live in modernity in which one unfolds their stories to build identity by deciding how to behave and what to wear by oneself. In particular, crossing the boundaries not only of geography and culture, but also of the public/private and business/home spheres in search of progress, Lucy and Margaret are appropriate to the changing modernity. Jane once attempts and witnesses herself in transition but finally finds her happiness in domestic life that is still different from one of dependent middle-class women. Indeed, modernised environments and new mobile cultures have changed individual perceptions, values, and assessments of the world into those full of diversity.

Works Cited

Text

Brontë, Charlotte. *Jane Eyre* (1847), edited by Stevie Davies. Penguin, 2006.

——. *Villette* (1853), edited by Herbert Rosengarten and Margaret Smith. Oxford University Press, 2008.

Gaskell, Elizabeth. *North and South* (1854). Edited by Patricia Ingham. Penguin, 2003.

Works Cited

Adey, Peter. *Mobility*. Routledge. 2010.

Anderson, Perry. "Modernity and Revolution" *New Life Review*, 144, 1984, pp. 96–113.

Athmanathan, Divya. "'You might pioneer a little at home': Hybrid Spaces, Identities and Homes in Elizabeth Gaskell's *North and South*." *Place and Progress in the Works of Elizabeth Gaskell*, edited by Lesa Scholl, Emily Morris, and Sarina Gruver Moore, Farnham, Surry and Burlington, Ashgate, 2015, pp. 37–52.

Bachmann-Medick, Doris. *Cultural Turns: New Orientations in the Study of Culture*. Translated by Adam Blauhut, De Gruyter, 2016.

Bagwell, Philip. *The Transport Revolution from 1770*. Batsford, 1974.

Beard, George. "Causes of American Nervousness." In *Popular Culture and Industrialism*, edited by Henry Nash Smith. New York University Press, 1967, pp. 57–70.

Berman, Marshall, *All That is Solid Melts into Air: The Experience of Modernity*, Verso, 1983.

Bhabha, Homi. "The Third Space: Interview with Homi Bhabha." *Identity: Community, Culture, Difference*, edited by Jonathan Rutherford, Lawrence and Wishart, 1990.

Burroughs, Robert. "Gaskell on the Waterfront: Leisure, Labor, and Maritime Space in the Mid-Century." *Place and Progress in the Works of Elizabeth Gaskell*, edited by Lesa Scholl and Emily Morris, Burlington, Ashgate (Routledge), 2015, pp. 11–22.

Butler, Judith. *Gender Trouble: Feminism and the Subversion of Identity.* Routledge, 1990.

Cresswell, Tim. *On The Move: Mobility in the Modern Western World.* Routledge, 2006.

Davidoff, Leonore, and Catherine Hall. *Family Fortunes: Men and Women of the English Middle Class, 1780–1850.* University of Chicago Press, 1987.

Dennis, Abigail. "Mobile Narrative, Spatial Mediation, and Gaskell's Urban Rustics in *North and South*." *MHRA Working Papers in the Humanities*, no. 4, 2009, pp. 43–54.

Elden, Stuart, Elizabeth Lebas, and Eleonore Kofman, eds. *Henri Lefebvre: Key Writings.* Continuum, 2003.

Elliott, Dorice Williams. *The Angel out of the House: Philanthropy and Gender in Nineteenth-Century England.* University Press of Virginia, 2002.

Ellis, Kate Ferguson. *The Contested Castle: Gothic Novels and the Subversion of Domestic Ideology.* University of Illinois Press, 1989.

Felski, Rita. "The Invitation of Everyday Life." *New Formation*, 39, 1999, pp. 15–31.

Fraiman, Susan. "Jane Eyre's Fall from Grace." *Jane Eyre*, Bedford, 1996, pp. 614–31.

Friedman, Susan Stanford. "Periodizing Modernism: Postcolonial Modernities and the Space/Time Borders of Modernist Studies" in *Modernism/modernity*, vol 13. 3, 2006, pp. 425–43.

Foucault, Michel. "The Eye of Power." *Power/Knowledge*. Pantheon, 1980, pp. 146–65.

———. *Discipline and Punish: The Birth of the Prison.* 1975. Penguin, 1991.

———. "Of Other Spaces." *The Visual Culture Reader.* 2nd edition, edited by Nicholas Mirzoeff, Routledge, 1998, pp. 237–44.

Giddens, Anthony. *Modernity and Self-Identity: Self and Society in the Late Modern Age.* Polity Press. 1991.

Gilbert, Sandra. M., and Susan Gubar. *The Madwoman in the Attic: The Woman Writer and the Nineteenth-Century Literary Imagination.* Yale University Press, 1979.

Gordon, Eleanor, and Gwyneth Nair. *Public Lives: Women, Family, and Society in Victorian Britain.* Yale University Press, 2003.

Hanks, P. (ed.) *Collins Dictionary of the English Language.* Collins, 1979.

Heller, Tamar and Patricia Moran, eds. *Scenes of the Apple: Food and the Female Body in Nineteenth- and Twentieth-Century Women's Writing*. State University of New York Press, 2003.

Hoeveler, Diane Long. *Gothic Feminism: The Professionalization of Gender from Charlotte Smith to the Brontë*. Pennsylvania State University Press, 1998.

Horrocks, Ingrid. *Women Wanderers and the Writing of Mobility, 1784–1814*. Cambridge University Press, 2017.

Ingham, Patricia. *The Language of Gender and Class: Transformation in the Victorian Novel*. Routledge, 1996.

Jacobus, Mary. "The Buried Letter: Feminism and Romanticism in *Villette*." *Women Writing and Writing about Women*, Croom Helm Ltd., 1979.

Jakubowski, Zuzanna. *Moors, Mansions, and Museums*. Berlin, Peter Lang Verlag, 2021.

Lambert, Carolyn. *The Meanings of Home in Elizabeth Gaskell's Fiction*. Victorian Secrets, 2013.

Lefebvre, Henri. *The Production of Space*. Blackwell, 1991.

Livesey, Ruth. *Writing the Stage Coach Nation: Locality on the Move in Nineteenth-Century British Literature*. Oxford University Press, 2016.

Logan, Thad. *The Victorian Parlour*. Cambridge University Press, 2001.

Macfarlane, Robert. *Mountains of the Mind: Adventures in Reaching the Summit*. Knopf, 2004.

Massey, Doreen. *Space, Place and Gender*. Polity, 1994.

Mathieson, Charlotte. *Mobility in the Victorian Novel: Placing the Nation*. Palgrave Macmillan, 2015.

McDowell, Linda. *Gender, Identity and Place, Understanding Feminist Geographies*. Polity Press, 1999.

Monahan, Melodie. "Heading Out Is Not Going Home: Jane Eyre." *Studies in English Literature*, 28, 1988, pp. 589–608.

Morgan, Simon. *A Victorian Woman's Place: Public Culture in the Nineteenth Century*. Tauris Academic Studies, 2007.

Morrison, Lucy. "Brontëan Reveries of Spaces and Places: Walking in Villette." *Time, Space, and Place in Charlotte Brontë*, edited by Diane Long Hoeveler, Deborah Denenholz Morse, Routledge, 2017.

Moers, Ellen. *Literary Women*. Oxford University Press, 1977.

Mullen, Mary. "In Search of Shared Time: National Imaginings in Elizabeth Gaskell's *North and South*." *Place and Progress in the Works of Elizabeth Gaskell*. Edited by Lesa Scholl, Emily Morris, and Sarina Gruver Moore, Farnham, Surry and Burlington, Ashgate, 2015, pp. 107–19.

Parkins, Wendy. *Mobility and Modernity in Women's Novels, 1850s-1930s: Women Moving Dangerously*. Palgrave Macmillan, 2009.

———. "Women, Mobility and Modernity in Elizabeth Gaskell's *North and South*." *Women's Studies International Forum*, 27. 5–6, 2004, pp. 507–19.

"Pastoral," def. A. 1. *Collins English Dictionary*, https://www.collinsdictionary. com/jp/dictionary/english/pastoral. Accessed 23 September 2022.

Piehler, Liana F. *Spatial Dynamics and Female Development in Victorian Art*. Peter Lane, 2003.

Plasa, Carl. *Charlotte Brontë*. Palgrave Macmillan, 2004.

Poovey, Mary. *Uneven Developments: The Ideological Work of Gender in Mid-Victorian England*. University of Chicago, 1988.

Rutherford, Jonathan. "The Third Space: Interview with Homi Bhabha." *Identity: Community, Culture, Difference*, edited by Jonathan Rutherford, Lawrence, and Wishart, 1990, pp. 207–21.

Scholl, Lesa. "Moving Between *North and South*: Cultural Signs and the Progress of Modernity in Elizabeth Gaskell's Novel." *Place and Progress in the Works of Elizabeth Gaskell*, edited by Lesa Scholl, Emily Morris, and Sarina Gruver Moore, Farnham, Surry and Burlington, Ashgate, 2015, pp. 95–105.

Senf, Carol. "Charlotte Brontë's *Jane Eyre* and the personal politics of space." *Time, Space, and Place in Charlotte Brontë*, edited by Diane Long Hoeveler, Deborah Denenholz Morse, Routledge, 2017.

Shuttleworth, Sally. "Introduction." *Jane Eyre*, by Charlotte Brontë. Oxford University Press, 2000, pp. vii–xxxiii.

Spain, Daphne. *Gendered Spaces*. University of North Carolina P, 1992.

Stoneman, Patsy. *Elizabeth Gaskell*. Manchester University Press, 2006.

Tanner, Tony. Introduction. *Villette*, by Charlotte Brontë. Penguin, 1979, pp. 7–51.

Tange, Andrea Kaston. *Architectural Identities: Domesticity, Literature, and the Victorian Middle Class*. University of Toronto Press, 2010.

Urry, John. *Mobilities*. Polity Press. 2007.

Wallace, Anne D. *Walking, Literature, and English Culture: The Origins and Uses of Peripatetic in the Nineteenth Century*. Clarendon Press, 1983.

Weisman, Leslie Kanes. *Discrimination by Design: A Feminist Critique of the Man-Made Environment*. University of Illinois Press, 1992.

"Whitewash." *Oxford Learner's Dictionary*, 2022, https://www.oxfordlearnersdictionaries.com/definition/english/whitewash_1.Accessed 23 September 2022.

Wolfreys, Julian. *Transgression: Identity, Space, Time*. Palgrave Macmillan, 2008.

Mobility, Modernity, and Space
in
Jane Eyre, *Villette*, and *North and South*

2024年9月10日　初版発行

著　者　　石井　麻璃絵

発行者　　福岡　正人

発行所　　株式会社　金　星　堂

（〒101–0051）東京都千代田区神田神保町 3–21
　　　　　Tel. (03)3263–3828（営業部）
　　　　　　　(03)3263–3997（編集部）
　　　　　Fax (03)3263–0716
　　　　　https://www.kinsei-do.co.jp

©2024 石井麻璃絵
組版／ほんのしろ　装丁デザイン／岡田知正
印刷所／モリモト印刷　製本所／松島製本
落丁・乱丁本はお取り替えいたします
本書の内容を無断で複写・複製することを禁じます

ISBN978-4-7647-1235-5 C1098
Printed in Japan